TO FEAR HIM

A LAKE DISTRICT THRILLER

DI SAM COBBS
BOOK 15

M A COMLEY

To my mother, gone but never forgotten. Miss you every second of every day, Mum.

Also to my dear friend, Mary, I hope you found the peace you were searching for, lovely lady.

ACKNOWLEDGMENTS

Special thanks as always go to @studioenp for their superb cover design expertise.

My heartfelt thanks go to my wonderful editor Emmy, my proofreaders Joseph and Barbara for spotting all the lingering nits.

A special shoutout to all my wonderful ARC Group, who help to keep me sane.

TO FEAR HIM

M A COMLEY

PROLOGUE

At the end of a long day, all Emily Burke wanted was to go home and put her feet up, except that wasn't on the cards, not this evening.

"So, are you going anywhere nice tonight?" Simon, her prying colleague on the nearby desk, asked. "Don't tell me you're already dating again."

"And what if I was? What would that have to do with you?"

"Charming. There's no need to snap my head off. It was a genuine question, that's all. Keep your little secret close to your chest, then. Nothing new there."

She pulled a face at him. "Aww, have I upset you? You're probably more disappointed because I won't share details about my love life, rather than being upset that I asked you to mind your own business. Am I right?"

Simon crossed his arms in defiance and glared at her. "Absolute bullshit. Pardon me for showing an interest in you. It won't happen again. You've been a frigging pain in the arse around here for months, and I'm not the only one who has noticed it, either. Sneaking off here and there on your clandestine meetings, keeping everyone in the dark upon your return, expecting us to cover your arse when the boss comes looking for you. Well, no more." He brushed his hands together. "I've had enough of your attitude. You know what you need, lady?"

"No, but I'm sure you're going to tell me, what with you being the wisest man in this office, who knows everything there is to know about what a woman desires, Simon."

He snarled and grumbled, "To get laid."

Emily tried hard to hold in the laughter, but despite her best efforts, a snigger slipped out. She should have expected what he was about to say. All the man ever talked about was sex, to the extent that it had become tedious beyond words. "Give it a rest," she said, eager to slap him down. "There's more to life than sex, in case you haven't realised."

"Maybe in your world, love, not in mine."

"And there we have it, the one major difference between us. Or should I say, between men and women?"

"Hey, speak for yourself," Fearne shouted across the room, earwigging their conversation.

She refused to retaliate and flashed a toothy smile instead. Then she picked up her handbag and left the office. "See you all tomorrow."

Exiting the building of *The Workington Herald*, she inhaled a large breath of fresh air, which always put right the wrongs she'd encountered during a long day. She loved her job, she truly did, but sometimes the people surrounding her in the office made it a chore to come here every day. Emily was one of the best investigative journalists on the paper but had been really struggling over the last few months, which had coincided with her husband filing for divorce behind her back. She had been so wrapped up in a case that had been consuming her lately that she'd failed to notice there was anything wrong with her marriage.

A few months ago, Gerald had prepared the evening meal as usual and served it up at the kitchen table, along with the divorce papers. He hadn't made a scene, which surprised the hell out of

Emily because once she'd opened the letter, that's exactly what she did in response to it.

Emily shook the image from her mind and crossed the road to her car. She drove home, knowing that there would be no one there to greet her. That was fine with her. She had handled the rejection remarkably well, in her opinion, not shedding a tear in front of Gerald. He had moved out within a week of serving her with the papers. She wasn't sure where he was staying, he hadn't left her a forwarding address, but she had an inkling, despite him assuring her otherwise, that he was shacked up with another woman. Looking back over the last couple of months of their marriage, she realised all the warning signs were there.

She arrived home ten minutes later and ran a bath, during which she soaked away the day's stresses, and she even contemplated calling off the night out she had planned with her friends later.

"Nope, I need this. I need to get out there again, to be normal rather than sitting at home all night, working, letting my imagination run away from me."

Her mobile rang. "Hi, Amy. If you're checking up on me, I told you not to worry. I'll be there at eight, as planned."

Amy laughed. "Me checking up on you, would I?"

"Yes, you would. I'm looking forward to meeting up with you all this evening. I know I've been unsociable lately. It hasn't been intentional, I promise. See you later."

"That's great to hear. We're dying to know what you've been up to."

"We'll see. Bye for now." She chewed her lip and remained in the bath for another five minutes, doubting if she was ready to share with her friends the latest case she'd been working on. It was bad enough being ridiculed by her colleagues at work, let alone her friends, telling her how dangerous the situation could be if she made the wrong move.

After washing her hair, she emptied the water, dried herself, and then came the onerous chore of deciding what to wear for the evening at the pub. She let out a relieved sigh it was only the pub they were going to. Some of her friends had tried to persuade her that letting her hair down at a nightclub would be the answer to her problems, but secretly, she couldn't think of anything worse. Thankfully, Amy came down on her side and refused to go the extra mile, especially during the week. Amy had blamed the fact that her tyrant of a boss was making extra demands on her because they were launching a new product line at the factory. She was a secretary and often had to contend with listening to her boss whinging, which she was finding more and more tedious every day. Emily had tried taking Amy to one side, told her she was too good for her boss and encouraged her to seek a different job elsewhere. She'd even told Amy to apply for an admin job at the paper Emily worked for, but Amy wasn't one for accepting changes or new challenges with open arms.

After drying her long brown hair, she went over to her wardrobe to search for something suitable to wear. Catching her eye were her smart black trousers and the red blouse she had bought the week before from the catalogue. She stared at her reflection from every angle, unsure whether or not the blouse suited her. Seconds later, she tore it off. "Nope, I don't like it. I'll send that back at the weekend. I was foolish to think I could get away with such a plunging neckline with these boobs." She hunted through her wardrobe again and chose her khaki top, or her *Old Faithful*, as she preferred to call it.

She caught a taxi into town and met up with the girls outside The Admiral's Arms. Everyone was in high spirits, and they ordered an assortment of cocktails from the bar. Amy and Emily were the ones who distributed the drinks.

Before anyone could start a conversation, Amy announced, "I can't stay too long tonight. My boss is being more and more demanding lately, which means I've been going in earlier every day."

"I hope he's paying you extra for the inconvenience," Emily said. She could tell by the way Amy's gaze dropped to her drink that wasn't the case. "You're hopeless. I've told you before, he's taking the piss. You need to change that and find a boss who will treat you right."

"I agree," the others said in unison.

"I know what you all think, but the familiarity of my position is key here. I don't think I could even consider changing jobs now."

"What?" Emily screeched. "Why not? Don't tell me you think your age is against you. You're thirty-two, not fifty-two, for Christ's sake."

The others chipped in, adding to Amy's frustration. "Emily is right. You're too young not to want more out of life and from your career," Penny said.

"Oh, please, don't make this evening about me and my boring life. Come on, Emily, we want to know what story you've been covering lately. You're the one whose career keeps us on the edge of our seats."

"As it happens, I'm working on something major, and yes, that's all you're going to get out of me about it. There's a long way to go before I can reveal what I've uncovered about this crazy, hateful individual."

"Bloody tease," Halima chastised and took a swig from her mojito.

"I know. Believe me, I'm itching to reveal all. There's just a tiny little piece to the puzzle that I need to find first. Hey, if it's any consolation, you guys will be the first to know."

"God, how many times have we heard you tell us that over the years?" Rachel said with a shake of her head.

"Honestly, it's an enormous story. I can't possibly reveal anything yet."

"Okay, we trust you," Rachel said. "Can't you give us a teeny-weeny morsel to be going on with?"

Emily rolled her eyes and sighed. "All I'm prepared to tell you is that it's disgusting, immoral and, no, I can't say anything else. Does anyone want a top-up?"

"I'll get them," Penny was the first to offer.

"I'd better make this my last one," Amy muttered.

"You're kidding me. It's barely nine o'clock," Halima complained. "What's the point in us getting all glammed up just for one or two cocktails? Yes, I'm putting my foot down, Amy. You're going to stay with us until the end."

Amy turned to face Emily, seeking help. Emily shrugged. "One night isn't going to hurt, sweetheart. We could all do with letting our hair down. It's been a while since we found the time to get together. Who knows when our next night out is going to be?"

Reluctantly, Amy agreed, and they ended up staying another couple of hours, sinking a few extra cocktails during that time. They said farewell when the bar manager announced last orders. Amy and Emily waved the other girls off and walked for a while. Emily had a raging headache and was uncharacteristically unsteady on her feet.

"Are you sure you want to walk? You don't look too good, hon. We should get a taxi here. It makes more sense picking one up from the rank rather than chancing our luck later."

"Oh God, I feel like I'm going to puke all the time. I can't see a driver being happy with me if I did that in the back of his car. I just need to take in some fresh air for a while. You get a taxi. I'll be fine if you want to leave me."

Amy hooked her arm through hers. "No way am I leaving you in this state. What the heck were you drinking tonight?"

"Same as usual. I suppose it's been a while since I necked a few bevvies." Emily tried to stand upright. She had griping pains in her stomach, and her legs refused to co-operate, not allowing her to walk in a straight line.

"Jesus, you're getting worse, not better. Are you sure you don't want me to call us a cab?"

"Maybe we should. Wait, we'll hail one down soon."

"Okay, if you insist. Here, give me your arm. I'll help to hold you upright. Did you eat before coming out this evening?"

Amy wrapped Emily's arm around her shoulder. "I don't know, I can't remember. Hang on, no, I don't think I did. That's probably what the problem is. I could do with a kebab, if there's one around here."

"There isn't. They're all in the opposite direction."

A car pulled up alongside them, and the driver lowered his window. "Evening, ladies. Can I be of service to anyone?"

It was too dark to see the driver. "Come on, let's get in, Emily. I don't think it's safe for us to be out here alone."

"Okay, you win."

Amy opened the back door of the car and placed Emily in the

back seat. The driver screeched away from the kerb. Everything was a blur after that for Emily. Within seconds, she passed out.

THE DRIVER STARED at the woman in his rear-view mirror, gesticulating in the middle of the road. She was getting on his nerves. Knowing what he had to do, he reversed into one of the side roads and headed back towards the incensed woman. She remained in the middle of the road, waving her arms wildly at him. He put his foot down on the accelerator and aimed straight at her. She was too drunk to get out of the way and avoid the impact.

Laughing, he struck her and sent her spinning onto the pavement. He drove away from the scene and pulled over once he was out of view, just in case there were any witnesses he hadn't noticed hanging around. He checked the back seat. Emily was out cold and none the wiser. He rubbed his hands together, delighted that the drugs he'd spiked her drink with had been successful.

Then he drove to the house he was using for the next six months, his parents' home, while they were off on their jollies in Spain. He'd been planning this for months, along with the other things that had kept him occupied. He was aware of who Emily was and that she'd been closing in on him. He knew it was important to deal with her, abduct her before she took the evidence he suspected she had on him to the police.

He was over the moon to have finally grabbed the bitch. She'd outsmarted him several times in the last couple of weeks. He knew that her husband had moved out of the marital home, and he'd jumped on the opportunity to make his move this evening after overhearing a conversation over the phone at work between Amy and Emily, planning a night out together with a few of their other friends. He'd hung around the reception area to hear their plans and came up with the idea of spiking Emily's drink as he passed her table.

Earlier that evening, he'd waited until some of the other girls had gone to the toilet and Emily was deep in conversation with someone on the table behind her. Then he'd made his move, successfully adding the drug to her drink. Watching in the shadows, he saw the effects of the drug taking over and pounced when he realised she and Amy would be walking home when the others had all chosen to take a taxi.

He crawled along behind them for a while to ensure they were going the right way and then parked up, waiting for his chance to appear. He could tell the drug was having the desired effect on Emily and stepped in to help. Now he had her where he wanted her and had no intention of letting her go in the near future.

Laughing, he reprimanded himself and checked his hostage once more. She was out for the count.

He arrived at the house and checked the lights at the other properties around him—they were all out, indicating it was safe to move his captive. He opened the back door, pulled her upright, then eased her over his shoulder, relieved that she was lighter than he'd assumed her to be. He entered the house and took her down to the cellar, where he'd built a couple of soundproof rooms for his parents over the past few months, under the pretence that he wanted to play his music down there rather than disturb them in the main part of the house, even though he lived elsewhere.

Luckily, his parents had agreed, and he'd built a total of three further rooms.

Now all he had to do was fill them with unsuspecting women.

1

Detective Inspector Sam Cobbs watched her fiancé, Rhys, prepare his packed lunch in the kitchen of their small cottage. Sonny and Casper, their two dogs, were sitting at his feet, awaiting the scraps he kept intentionally dropping on the floor beside him.

"Don't you dare complain to me about them begging at the dinner table."

He cast a glance over his shoulder and smirked. "I wouldn't dream of it. Some scraps here and there won't hurt them."

Sam flashed him one of her warning looks and shook her head. She was wary about pushing the topic too far, aware of how fragile he still was after the savage attack he'd suffered a few months ago. He was getting there, almost eighty percent back to normal. She was definitely having to choose her battles with him for fear of upsetting him. This was something new he was dealing with, going back to work, and choosing to take a packed lunch with him instead of stepping out of his office, as that's when the attack had occurred and a thug stabbed him.

"Are you sure you're up to going back? The doctor has only just given you the all-clear."

"You worry too much. I can't sit around here for months on end, bleeding you dry, expecting you to cover all the bills. For one thing, I have my pride to consider."

Sam knew there would be no point in arguing with him. She'd noticed the improvement in him daily, especially over the last fortnight. She admitted defeat and held her hands up. "Okay, but promise me that the moment you feel things getting on top of you, you call it a day and come home."

"I promise. Brenda virtually told me the same. I'm in safe hands with her as my secretary. She's a carbon copy of you where my health is concerned. She told me you rang her last week." He wagged a finger at her. "Naughty girl, going behind my back."

"I didn't, not really. It was with good intentions and without malice, I promise you."

He finished making his sandwich and placed it in the Tupperware box, then put all the ingredients he'd used to fill it back in the fridge. Afterwards, he took a step towards her and gathered her in his arms. "I'm going to be all right. The longer I stay off work, the harder it's going to be getting back in the saddle. All I'll be doing is letting my patients down, and you know how long it has taken me to build up that business."

"I know. I'm worried about you. There's no harm in that, is there?"

"You're too sweet. Honestly, I'm fine. I'll shout if I need to hear your reassuring words to brighten my day, how's that?"

She smiled, and then she kissed him. Casper and Sonny both barked and jumped up, keen to be included in the cuddle. Sam ruffled their heads. "I suppose we should take these two out for a quick walk. I bet Casper is looking forward to going with you to the office today. I wonder if he realises what's going on."

"He's too smart not to understand something different is about to happen. I can do the honours if you're running behind schedule."

Sam glanced at the clock on the wall. It was coming up to eight-thirty. "We're both going to be late at this rate. Maybe we should just whip them around the block instead of taking them to the park like we usually do."

"I'm up for it, if you are."

They hurriedly gathered the boys' leads and set off. When they returned, their neighbour, Doreen, was standing at her lounge window, waving at them.

"I'll be two minutes," Sam mouthed to her dear friend. "Now that's one person whose day is about to get a lot brighter."

"Definitely."

Sam entered the house and tore around the kitchen, preparing Sonny's and Casper's individual bags of goodies for the day. Then she took Sonny next door to be with Doreen.

"How wonderful to have my favourite pup with me again. I must ask, and I hope you don't find my question nosey. How is Rhys doing now? Far from me to interfere, but are you sure he's well enough to go back to work? It seems a tad early to me."

Sam hugged and kissed her remarkable ageing neighbour on the cheek and closed the front door behind her. They walked into the lounge before she replied, "Between you and me, yes, I think it's too early, as well, however, he's adamant he wants to face the world and, more importantly, to earn money again."

"Oh my, if that's all it is about, I have some money tucked away that you're welcome to borrow, rather than him risking his health like that."

"That's super sweet of you to offer, Doreen, but I fear if I told him, it would only make him more determined to get back in the office."

"Oh gosh. What a situation to find yourselves in, Sam. I feel for you, my dear. Is he going to take Casper with him?"

"Yes, he's just prepared a packed lunch for himself. To be honest with you, I'm glad he's going to stay in the office and not venture out at lunchtime."

"That's all well and good, taking his lunch with him, but Casper will need to go out. He won't be able to keep his legs crossed all day."

"I know. Perhaps he's been training the pup to use the toilet to prepare for this day arriving."

They both laughed.

"Oh my, don't say that. Wouldn't it be marvellous if people could do it? What a scream that would be!"

"I'm sure I've seen some clips on social media over the years where people have trained their dogs to do just that."

"Never! Well, they say it takes all sorts to make up this world of ours, so nothing should really surprise us, should it?"

"Absolutely. Anyway, how have you been lately?"

"I'm okay. I've been missing Sonny much more than I thought I would. I know I can see him any time I like. It's not the same, though, as having him here with me, sitting by my side. He's such an incredible source of comfort to me during the day."

Sam's eyes misted up. "Sweetheart, you should have said. He's as much your dog as he is ours. Anytime you want him to keep you company, all you have to do is give us a shout. And, let me reiterate, you know you're welcome to pop round to our place when you want. You don't need a special invitation to come and see us."

"Thank you, Sam. That means a lot to me. I'm going to be making a chicken casserole for later, if you'd both like to join me?"

Sam smiled. "You're too kind. We'd love to." She hoped accepting the thoughtful invitation wouldn't upset Rhys when she told him. "I'm going to have to fly now, otherwise, I'll be late for work." She handed over the bag containing Sonny's lunch and a few treats, then kissed her beloved cockapoo goodbye. "Be good, no playing Auntie Doreen up, you hear me?"

Sonny licked her face and dutifully sat beside Doreen and nudged her hand to pet him.

"Don't worry, I won't allow him to misbehave."

Sam cocked an eyebrow. "Why don't I believe you?"

Doreen winked and smiled. "It's a shame we haven't got time to debate if I'm telling the truth or not. Maybe you can interview me later, over dinner. How does six-thirty sound to you?"

"If you're sure that time is acceptable to you?"

Doreen nodded.

"Then it sounds fine to me, to us. Have a good day, and don't let him run rings around you."

"Yes, boss. Now, shoo, we'll be fine, won't we, handsome?" Doreen stroked Sonny's fluffy head. He gazed up at her, his mouth opening into the perfect smile. "Look at him. He's just adorable."

"He's tugging at my heart. Right, I'm off before I decide to call in sick for the day and join you two."

"You'll do no such thing. This town needs you to protect us."

"I'm going. Ring me if you have any problems during the day, and thank you, Doreen."

"Get away with you. I have my little pal back with me. What could go wrong?"

Sam cringed, hoping that Doreen hadn't tempted fate. "See you later. Have a fun day, the pair of you."

She left the house, exited the garden and entered her own. By this time, Doreen and Sonny were standing at the lounge window, waving her off. She blew them both a kiss and opened the front door. Rhys was in the hallway, looking petrified.

"Hey, what's wrong?"

He paced the small area. Casper, too, seemed unnerved by the situation and moved out of the way to sit beside Sam.

"I don't know if I can do it," Rhys whispered, his voice trembling.

Sam sighed and stepped forward to comfort him, or to distract him from pacing. He pulled out of her grasp and sweat broke out on his forehead. "Rhys, you're going to need to calm down. So what if you delay your return for a few days? No one would blame you for postponing or cancelling their appointments. Everyone understands the trauma you've been through. What did Meredith say? Does she think you're ready for this yet?"

His head lowered, and he shook it. "No, I'm going against her advice going back this soon."

"There you are then. How would you feel if one of your patients went against your advice? Why don't you give Meredith a call, see if you can book an appointment for during the day?"

"No, she's away on holiday at the moment. I wouldn't want to disturb her."

"Hey, I'm sure she won't mind." She rubbed his upper arms, and his shaking instantly died down. "You're working yourself up into a state for no reason. I've told you, I can handle the bills. Your health is more important, love."

She opened her arms, and he walked into them. Then he did the thing she least expected. He broke down and cried. Something he'd failed to do during his recuperation, so she knew how bad the situation must be for him.

"There, there, everything is going to be just fine. Let it out. You've been holding it in for far too long."

"I'm sorry. I... I don't know what I'd do without you, Sam, that's the God's honest truth. You really mean the world to me."

She gently pushed him away and lifted his chin with her finger. "We'd be lost without each other. That's why I agreed to marry you. I'll always be here for you, Rhys. Don't shut me out."

"I'm not, at least not intentionally. Maybe I'll take another day off today and prepare myself for going into battle again tomorrow, instead."

"Sounds like an excellent idea to me. I have another one to add to the mix. Why don't you leave it for a couple of hours, then go for a hike with the dogs? That'll give you the time to get your mind in the right place. I'm sure Doreen won't mind you taking Sonny off her hands for a while. Oh, and she's invited us for dinner this evening."

His eyes widened. "I'm not sure if I'm ready for that, Sam."

"It's Doreen. Come on, it'll do us both the world of good to have a night off from cooking. It would mean so much to her to have our company this evening."

He hesitated for a moment or two and then let out a deep sigh. "Okay, if you think that's the right thing to do."

She winked at him. "You listen to the inspector, who knows what's right and what's wrong in this world."

He smiled, and Sam spotted a glimmer of the old sparkle back in his eyes. "I'll call Brenda and ask her to postpone my appointments, then head over to Ennerdale with the boys."

"Oh crap, did you have to tell me where you're going? That's going to bug me for the rest of the day now. You know how much I love that place."

"Sorry, you could always pull a sickie yourself."

"Sorry, as much as I'd love to, it's just not in me to do it. Why don't you drop in and say hi to Emma and the gang at The Gather? You could grab a bacon roll or something at the end of your walk."

"I'm not sure if I'm up to it. I'll see later."

Sam glanced at her watch and cursed under her breath. "I'm sorry, I'm going to have to go, or I'll get caught up in the rush-hour traffic. We both know what that's like in Workington."

"Go, I'll be fine. One meltdown a day is usually my limit."

She hugged and kissed him. "I'm always here for you, whether or not I'm at work. Call me if you need to chat, all right?"

"I will. I promise. Have a good day."

"Want me to pop back and tell Doreen what you have planned for the day?"

"No, I'll go round and have a coffee with her in a little while, once I've rung the office and spoken with Brenda. Thanks, Sam."

She smiled and waved her hand. "For what? I have done nothing special."

"You did, you just don't realise it. Have a good day."

"I will. Don't forget to call me if you need me."

"I won't."

They shared another kiss, then Sam bent down to kiss Casper. "You take care of your dad for me, got that?"

Casper licked her face in response.

"Right, I'd better get a move on. Love you. Take care and enjoy your day. Take plenty of photos."

"I will. I love you, too, Sam, more than you will ever know."

IN THE END, Sam made it to work by the skin of her teeth. She'd been forced to take a shortcut to avoid the heaviest of the traffic and got stuck behind a lorry unloading down one of the side streets that delayed her a few extra minutes. She rang ahead and warned Bob, her partner, that she might be late because of unforeseen circumstances. He'd ribbed her, and she'd ended up hanging up on him, not in the mood for his childish behaviour. Now she felt bad for the way she had treated him and, most of all, for being oversensitive.

She entered the reception area to find a perplexed Nick Travis, the desk sergeant, on duty. "Hey, I recognise that look. What's up?"

"I've been checking through the notes of what's happened overnight, ma'am, and something is standing out to me." He passed her a sheet of paper, which she cast a quick eye over.

"Damn, do you want me to chase it up?"

"I think someone should. I know it's not what you're usually used to dealing with."

Sam nodded. "But it could turn out to be something different."

"You read my mind."

"Can you run me a copy off, Nick?" She handed the piece of paper back to him and waited while he slipped into his office.

He returned and slid the sheet across the counter. "Thank you, ma'am. Will you let me know how you get on with the case?"

"Of course I will. I'll hold the morning meeting. There are a few details from the last case I need to go over with the team, and then I'll get on this straight away with Bob."

"I appreciate it. You know what it's like when you get a gut instinct about a case."

"I do. Leave it with me." She punched her code into the keypad and raced up the stairs. Bob was at his desk, a mug of coffee in his hand, talking with the rest of the team. He glanced her way and mumbled good morning. She passed his desk and uttered an apology.

After making herself a coffee, she said, "Listen up, folks. Nick has just had a word with me about an incident. I believe we should chase it up this morning. However, we need to briefly go over what's left for us to do on the Walcott case before it goes to court."

"I think all the i's have been dotted on that one," Bob piped up.

"Good, only you weren't too sure when I asked you at the end of our shift yesterday."

"What is this? Have a go at Bob day? If so, I must have missed that particular memo."

She cocked an eyebrow. "Are you for real?"

His gaze cast down to his desk, and he shrugged. "It's all covered, that's all I was saying."

"And that's all that needed to be said. Are you ready to go?"

He raised his mug. "I will be when I've finished this."

Sam took her mug and marched into her office, slamming the door behind her. She sensed by the time she'd drunk her coffee her mood would have improved considerably, and she'd be better prepared to tackle her partner, who was being more cantankerous than usual, which she could do without, given how her day had begun.

The door opened. "Knock, knock, can I come in?"

Sam glanced up from the email she was reading and stared at Bob. "Only if you promise to leave your foul mood on that side of the door."

He entered the office and closed the door behind him. "I'm not in a foul mood. You're the one who hung up on me earlier and tore me off a strip in front of the rest of the team."

"Bollocks." She ran her hand over her eyes. "I'm not in the mood for this, Bob. I have enough going on at home to deal with."

"Haven't we all? But some of us choose to leave our problems at home, instead of burdening our work colleagues."

"Get you! I wasn't burdening you with my problems. All I was asking for was a little leniency, like I've given you occasionally. Now, are you going to sit down and tell me what you want or not?"

"I'd rather stand." He approached the desk. "I've got some bad news to share."

Guilt draped around her shoulders, and at the same time a hand tightened around her heart. "You're not ill, are you?"

"Give me a chance to tell you before you jump to conclusions." He threw himself into the chair opposite her.

"Okay, I'm listening."

"It's Alex. He's got a bad ticker. His doctor has told him he needs a heart bypass. He asked me to break the news to you."

Sam bounced back in her chair. "Wow, I have to ask why he couldn't tell me himself."

"Do you really need me to answer that? You admitted yourself a while back that you didn't really get along with him. So why would he come to you?"

"Er... because I'm his frigging boss, that's why."

"He knows you've been under a lot of strain lately and didn't want to..."

"What? Burden me? That's what I'm here for. Get him in here, now."

His head lolled from one side to the other. "Don't do this. Why don't you have a chat with him later? Once the news has sunk in."

Sam sighed. "If you think that would be for the best. I'm mortified that he couldn't pluck up the courage to tell me himself. I hadn't realised the rift between us had got so bad."

"I don't think it has. He just felt more comfortable speaking to me about his health instead of you. You're not going to pull him over the coals for that, are you?"

"What do you take me for? I'm not an ogre, despite what you and the others might think." She tossed her biro across the room. "Is that what it's come to around here? My team going behind my back and coming to you with their problems?"

"Steady on. That's not the case at all, Sam. If you don't mind me saying, I think you're being a tad touchy about this matter."

"Possibly. Sod it. I've had enough of being in the office today. We need to get on the road. I'll deal with Alex and his bloody conflict-of-interest issues later, when I've calmed down."

"There you go again. Mountains and molehills come to mind, not for the first time lately."

Sam closed her eyes and sucked in a couple of deep breaths. She bit her tongue rather than upset Bob further.

. . .

They left the station and drove to the West Cumberland Hospital in Whitehaven. There, they asked the receptionist where Amy Yokes could be found.

"Let me check the system for you." The receptionist tapped the keys and came back with the answer almost immediately. "Here she is. Oh dear, she's in ICU, or what's known as the Critical Care Unit now. Do you know where that is?"

"We do. We've been there before. Will it be all right if we see her?"

"I wouldn't like to say. You'd be better off asking the nurses on the ward up there."

"We'll do that. Thank you for your help."

"My pleasure."

They hopped into the lift and rode it up to level three. There was a nurse talking to a doctor outside the ward. Sam produced her ID. "Hi, I'm Detective Inspector Sam Cobbs. I was hoping to have a chat with someone about Amy Yokes."

The doctor smiled and excused himself. "I'm Mandy, a nurse on the ward. Are you aware of what happened to her?"

"We're under the impression that Amy was knocked down last night. Can I ask how she is?"

"Not good. Her boyfriend and parents are in there with her, so I won't be able to let you in."

"No, no, that's fine. Obviously, we're going to need to speak with her family, but only when it's convenient for them."

"As you can imagine, they're beside themselves in there. I'll pop my head around the curtain, see if one of them will come out and have a word with you."

"That would be great. No pressure from us, though."

"I don't believe you. I dare say you'll be wanting to get on with the case and eager to find the person who did this to Amy."

Sam nodded. "It would help, although I appreciate how devastating this type of incident can be for a family to comprehend."

"I won't be long. Why don't you take a seat?"

"Thanks."

The nurse pushed through the door to the ward, and Sam and Bob took a seat on the plastic chairs close to the vending machine.

"Handy for when we need to have another cuppa." Bob grinned. "I'm kidding. Where's your sense of humour gone? And you haven't told me what's going on at home that is bringing you down."

With that, the door to the ward opened, and a man in his early thirties came towards them. "Are you the officers who have come to see us?"

Sam flashed her ID again. "DI Sam Cobbs, and this is my partner, DS Bob Jones, and you are?"

"Russell Lowe. I'm Amy's boyfriend; we actually live together. Her parents are in there. They're inconsolable. What can you tell us about the accident, if you can call it that?"

"There's nothing we can tell you about it at present. I wanted to drop by to introduce ourselves. My team will be running the investigation. I know it's not an ideal time to speak with Amy's parents, but perhaps you can help us? What can you tell us about the incident?"

He took a step back and ran a hand through his hair. "Nothing, not a damn thing. Amy went out last night with the girls and didn't come home. That's as much as I can tell you. Make of that what you will."

"Do you know where the accident happened?"

"It wasn't an accident. It was intentional. She was mowed down just for the sake of it and left there to die. Probably a drunk driver, scared of what would happen to him if the cops showed up. What are you going to do about it?"

"We're going to need to know where and when the incident took place. Who Amy was on a night out with. Where they went during the evening. If they had any trouble while they were out. That sort of thing. Will you be able to supply us with the information?"

He stared at Sam and tutted. "Bare minimum. You'd be better off speaking to her friends rather than being here, waiting for her to wake up, or expecting us to fill in the details for you."

"Can you give us her friends' numbers?"

He scratched his head and gazed at the wall over her shoulder.

"I wish I could. I just don't have the information. Wait, Emily is a journalist at the local paper. She should be easy for you to track down, shouldn't she?"

"That's great. I don't suppose you know her surname?"

"Hang on, let me think. It's similar to a comedienne's name... yes, that's it, Burke, like Kathy Burke."

"That's brilliant. Now, can you try to think of the other friends' names?"

After chewing on his lip for a few seconds, he replied, "I'm sorry. I can't think of any other names, not when my head is a mess, wondering if Amy is going to make it or not."

"I totally understand. I'm really not here to put you under any unnecessary pressure. If Emily is the only name you can recall, then that's fine. We'll see what we can find out. Perhaps you can tell me at what time she left the house yesterday?"

"Around eight, maybe slightly before. I was in the garage, tinkering with my kit car when she left."

"I see, thanks. We'll leave you to it now, unless you have any questions for us?"

"I can't think of anything. Is that it?"

"Yes, you've given us a name to go on. We'll see if we can find Emily. Perhaps she'll be able to answer any other questions we need to ask to get the investigation underway. Here's one of my cards, actually, here's another one. If you'd kindly pass it on to Amy's parents for me, maybe they can call me if they can think of anything, such as some of her other friends' names."

"I'll pass it on, but I wouldn't hold my breath. Their memories haven't been that reliable lately."

"Sorry to hear that. We'll be in touch with any information we find out. If Amy wakes up, will you give me a call?"

"You mean *when* she wakes up? I'm not ready to give up on her just yet."

"Sorry, of course I meant that."

"I'll ring you. Good luck with Emily." He turned on his heel and walked back into the ward before Sam had the chance to say goodbye.

On the way back to the car, she rang the station. "Claire, can you research the name Emily Burke for me? I have it on good authority that she works for the local newspaper. We're leaving the hospital now and will make our way over there, see if we can catch her in."

"Want me to look her up while you're on the line, boss?"

"Why not? Thanks, Claire."

Sam listened to Claire tapping at her keyboard.

"Ah yes, I thought I recognised the name. She's an investigative journalist on the paper. Made a name for herself a few years ago when she broke the story on that paedophile ring at one of the nurseries in the area."

"Yes, I remember. I think our paths have crossed several times over the years, but she's always kept her distance from me, never tried to hound me or interfere with any of the cases I've been involved in. I can't say that about her male counterparts, but the less said about that, the better."

Claire laughed. "Yeah, they can definitely be a pain in the arse for you. I'm checking out her Facebook page as we speak. The last post she made was several days ago. It was a meme about finally getting her life back on track."

"Does she mention if she's in a relationship with anyone?"

"Her relationship status is married. Let me see if I can find out who she's married to, just a sec... Yes, here it is, Gerald Burke. When I click on his name, it's coming up that he's an IT consultant with a computer firm called Freedom Electronics. I believe they're based out on the trading estate on the edge of Harrington."

"Excellent. Can you shoot the postcode over to me? We'll head over to the newspaper first to see if Emily is there and if she can tell us anything about last night. If you can stick with the social media side of things and see if you can source some of her friends' names, that would be great. Apparently, according to Amy's boyfriend, she went out at about eight last night intending to meet up with her friends and going into town for a drink."

"I'll keep on it, boss. How is she doing after the accident?"

"She's in ICU. We never got to see her. We've only managed to have a brief chat with her boyfriend. Her parents were also at the hospital, but they didn't leave her side. They were pretty distraught, which is understandable. We decided it would be best not to hang around there too long. We've reached the car. I'll be in touch soon."

"Okay, I'll keep checking both SM accounts and see what I can find."

2

Sam drove to *The Workington Herald* and parked outside the austere-looking building. She'd heard it was one of the oldest in the area, and it showed, at least on the outside. Inside, however, was a different story entirely. Sam and Bob crossed the light-coloured marble floor to the reception desk. Two women, one older, in her mid-forties, and the other in her late twenties, glanced up as they approached. Sam flashed her ID at the older woman.

"Hi, I'm DI Sam Cobbs. Is it possible to speak with Emily Burke?"

"May I ask what this is about?"

Sam spotted a name badge on the woman's chest. "It's personal, Cheryl. Is she available?"

Cheryl shifted in her seat and rang a number, then relayed the response she'd received from the person she'd spoken to. "I'm afraid she's not in today."

"May I ask why?"

Cheryl shrugged. "Your guess is as good as mine. That's what I was told before her colleague hung up."

"Is there someone in charge who we can speak to? It's important."

"Let me see if Mr Garrett has time to see you." She made the call and nodded. "You're in luck. Take the lift to the second floor. His office is at the end. His secretary will introduce you."

Sam smiled. "Thanks, that's great."

They headed towards the lift and waited for it to arrive.

"Strange that Emily isn't here," Bob said. He'd been quiet during their journey.

"I was thinking the same thing. Very strange indeed. I hope this won't be a wasted trip."

The lift door opened, and two men walked out. They eyed Sam and Bob cautiously as they passed.

"Tossers," Bob mumbled as they got into the lift.

Sam had trouble suppressing her laugh and dug him in the ribs with her elbow. "Behave yourself."

They followed the receptionist's directions and ended up outside the publishing manager's office door. Sam knocked on it, and a woman invited them to enter.

"Ah, we've been expecting you. Mr Garrett is on the phone at the moment. He shouldn't be long. Take a seat."

"Thanks."

They sat on the comfy chairs in the corner, and Sam picked up a glossy magazine to flick through.

She didn't get very far because the secretary said, "He's free if you want to go through."

"Thanks."

Bob reached the door first. He knocked and opened it. Sitting behind the desk was a man in his late fifties. He pushed his spectacles up into his thinning hair and gestured for them to take a seat.

"Come in. May I ask what this is about? I'm William Garrett, by the way."

"Nice to meet you. We came to have a chat with Emily Burke, but we were told she wasn't at work today. Do you know why?"

"I believe she's off for some reason or other. She hasn't rung in sick, she just hasn't shown up, which is unusual for her."

"Interesting. So she's usually dependable. Do you have a contact number for her?"

He dipped his head; his specs slipped back onto the bridge of his nose, and he opened a file on his computer, then jotted down a phone number and handed it across the table to Sam. "There you go, good luck trying to contact her, she's been ignoring my calls all morning. Which again is unlike her."

"Could there be something wrong?"

"You tell me. Wait, may I ask what your visit is about?"

"One of her friends was knocked down last night and is currently lying in ICU, fighting for her life."

"Shit. I hadn't heard. Oh Lordy, do you think this has anything to do with Emily not being at work today? Silly question. Forget I asked, it obviously the reason she's not here today, right?"

Sam shrugged. "It seems too much of a coincidence not to be connected. Did she come to work yesterday?"

"As far as I know. I'm only informed if a member of staff fails to show up for work. Do you want me to try calling her again?"

"That'd be great, if you wouldn't mind?"

"Of course." He dialled the number and put it on speaker. The phone rang four times before the voicemail kicked in. "Sorry, it's the only number we have on file for her. Most people choose not to have a house phone these days, don't they?"

"So it would seem. I wonder if it would be possible to speak with some of her work colleagues while we're here."

"I don't see why not. I'll take you over there myself. I could do with stretching my legs. My doctor is always lecturing me about sitting behind my desk all day without having intermittent exercise breaks."

They left the office and climbed the stairs at the end of the hallway to the next level. Garrett introduced Sam and Bob to the four people in the office they entered. A woman and three men stared back at them.

"The team will take care of you from here," Garrett said.

"Thanks for your help."

"What can we do for you?" the young woman asked.

Sam took a seat beside her. "And your name is?"

"I'm Fearne. I'm the general dogsbody around here. I'm the trainee journalist."

Sam nodded. "Okay, Fearne, what can you tell us about Emily Burke?"

"She's not here today. She never takes days off. I was worried about her when she didn't show up this morning, so I rang her only for her voicemail to kick in."

"When was the last time you saw her?"

"Yesterday. She told me she was going on a night out with friends. She even invited me along, but I declined. I'm a bit shy about meeting strangers."

"I can understand that. Did she tell you where she was going and who with?"

"Not really. She told me they were meeting up and heading into town for the evening. Has something happened to her?"

Sam lowered her voice. "I don't want this appearing in the news, not yet. It would seem that a friend she was with last night was involved in a hit-and-run. She's currently in the ICU, in a very bad way."

"Holy shit!" a man behind them said.

"All right, Simon, keep it down. And this is supposed to be a private conversation, so butt out."

"Get off your high horse, Fearne. This concerns all of us. We've known Emily longer than you."

"You'll get your chance to speak with the officers," Fearne snapped. "This is my time, moron."

Sam felt the need to intervene. "We don't want to cause any trouble. The more all of you can tell us, the better."

"She's a colleague who is well thought of around here," Fearne said. "She's excellent at her job, too, which can be the cause of some stress in the office."

"That's utter codswallop, Fearne," Simon shouted. "Tell it as it is or not at all. Stop making her out to be something she isn't."

Sam swivelled in her chair to face him. "If you've got something to say, say it."

"I haven't, not really. Except Emily is the type of woman who doesn't suffer fools gladly. If there's a story to be told, she gets down and dirty to bring that story to the public."

"Meaning? Was she working on something in particular?" Sam sensed she wasn't going to like the answer.

"We think so. It was all very cloak-and-dagger stuff, if you ask me. I tried to worm the information out of her a few times. She slapped me down and told me to keep my beak out."

"That's why we're journalists, because we're nosey and are keen to get to the bottom of things. That's how we make our living," Fearne said.

"So what's the problem, then?" Sam asked, perplexed and unsure where the conversation was heading.

"The problem is that even if the rest of us are up to our necks in it, we share what we're working on. Not Emily. Which, if you must know, drives the rest of us nuts."

"Hey, speak for yourself, mate," another man shouted across the room.

"Sod off, dipshit."

Simon dropped back into his seat, and Sam turned her attention back to Fearne.

"Is he right?"

"They don't really get along. They spend most of the day winding each other up, just for the sake of it. So what if she's secretive? She's learnt over the years that women have to work harder in this business. Emily more than most because of who her father is. He was an excellent journalist in his day. She has his talent for sniffing out a good story and keeping it close to her chest until all the facts are in place."

"I get that. I remember seeing her at some conferences I've held over the years. She wasn't one to stand out in the crowd but was always making notes."

"Methodical. That's her to a tee. She never reveals too much too soon about the cases she's working on."

"Does she keep ample notes? Perhaps type things up on the computer? Would it be worth us having a look on there?"

"Not unless you know her password. She always goes for obscure ones for obvious reasons, with the vultures circling, ready to swoop around here."

Sam peered over her shoulder, checking to see if Simon was still hovering, listening in to their conversation. He wasn't. "Do you think she's ticked anyone off around here enough for them to want to hurt her?"

"Oh shit! No, that thought never crossed my mind. I don't think so." She stood and looked over the glass barrier, shielding her from the rest of the team. "Simon's a royal pain in the arse, but I think, like most men, when it comes to the crunch, he lacks the balls to follow through on any threats he makes."

"Threats? Tell me more."

"Honestly, it's nothing. Like I said earlier, they're both as bad as one another, keen to rub each other up the wrong way, just to brighten their day. I think they like each other, really."

Sam raised an eyebrow, her interest piqued. "As in, you think there might be something going on between them?"

Fearne's eyes crinkled at the side, and she slapped a hand over her mouth. Eventually, she dropped her hand in her lap and said, "Oh God, no, nothing like that at all. More like sibling rivalry, I suppose. Definitely nothing romantic going on between them, perish the thought."

"Oops, sorry. Still, it gave you a laugh."

"And some. Seriously, I hope Emily going AWOL isn't to do with the story she's been working on. Then, if it is, that's the risk we take bringing heinous stories to the public. Emily is the best we have around here for doing that."

"I don't profess to know how journalists work when they're under pressure to perform. Does she have to disguise herself sometimes?"

Fearne collected the papers scattered around her desk and nodded. "Sometimes, when it's needed. The others refuse to do it. I'm inclined to agree with Emily. There are definitely times when such measures are called for, if only to keep ourselves safe."

"Do you have her address?"

"I roughly know where she lives, out at Stainburn, but I can't tell you her actual address, sorry."

"That's okay. I'll get my team to carry out the searches. Is there anything else you can tell us about her? Anything going on in her personal life, perhaps?"

Fearne placed a finger on her cheek as she thought. "I don't think so. No, hang on, she told me she was going through a divorce. She told me matter-of-factly a few months ago, and I didn't push the issue. I figured if she wanted to tell me more, she would, so I'm not sure if it has come through yet."

"I was aware she was married, however, not that she was going through a divorce. We'll look into that. Her husband is Gerald Burke, is that right?"

"Yes, that's correct. He's an IT whiz, apparently."

"Thanks. We know where he works. That was going to be our next call. How long have you worked alongside her?"

"I've been here around eighteen months. It would be tough for me around here if I didn't have her to rely on. She's taught me so much already, and I owe her a lot. I hope nothing bad has happened to her."

"We won't know until we find any evidence or clues. Since you've known her, has she hinted at having any problems? Sorry, just to be clearer, in the recent cases she's reported on, has anyone tackled her about something she's written about them?"

Fearne thought for a moment. "Nothing that I can think of, sorry."

"Don't be. You've been really helpful, thanks. We'd better chat with your colleagues now."

"Good luck with that."

THE CONVERSATIONS DIDN'T last long, especially the one with dear old Simon, who had already expressed his opinion about Emily. The other two men said they treated her like any other colleague, but she was very secretive about the stories she covered. They'd given Sam the impression Emily didn't trust those around her not to steal her leads. Nothing Sam or Bob heard triggered any warning signs from any of them.

They left and went back to the car.

"Let's visit the husband next. Hopefully, he can fill in a few blanks for us."

"I wouldn't be raising my hopes if I were you. Not if they've been separated for a couple of months."

"We'll see. Stop being so negative. It's not like we have anything else to go on, yet."

Freedom Electronics was in a unit on the trading estate. It was obvious that Gerald, despite his title as an IT consultant, did in fact run a one-man-band operation.

"Another bloke who likes to sound more important than he really is," Bob grumbled.

Sam punched him gently on the thigh. "Never judge a book by its cover, matey. We'll see what he has to say and then head back to the station."

"Maybe you'll be open to telling me what's going on at home on our way back to base."

She switched off the engine and winked at him. "You never know your luck. It's nothing major. Well, maybe it is."

Bob grunted. "Shut up and stop teasing."

"Okay." She grinned and exited the car.

Bob followed her and jumped ahead to open the door to the unit. A man in his early thirties looked up as they entered. He was using a magnifying glass, studying what appeared to be a circuit board for a computer.

He put his equipment down and stood. "Hello, I'm Gerald. How can I help you?"

"Ah, we were told you were an IT consultant."

"I am, but I like to keep my hands in with the practical side of things. I've been building computer packages for people for years." Frowning, he asked, "Are you after something in particular?"

Sam showed him her ID and introduced herself and her partner.

"The police? Has someone reported me?"

She held up a hand. "No, sorry. I suppose you'd call this a personal visit."

"Personal? I'm still not with you. Care to elaborate?"

"We're really here about your wife." She paused to assess his reaction.

His frown deepened. "My wife? Or soon-to-be ex-wife. What about her?"

"We're trying to find her."

"And you think I'll know where she is? Sorry to disappoint you, but we haven't spoken in about six to eight weeks. What do you mean you can't find her?"

"Just that. Her friend, Amy, is in the hospital and, as far as we're aware, Emily was with her last night, possibly when the accident happened."

"What? Is Amy all right?"

"She was involved in a hit and run. We've been to Emily's place of work, but she hasn't shown up today. Have you seen her?"

"No, like I said, not for six to eight weeks. You're worrying me now. I take it you've tried to call her, have you?"

"Yes, lots of people have tried and failed to get any response from her phone. It diverts to her voicemail straight away. That's why we're concerned."

He stepped back and rested his backside on the desk behind him. "I can't believe what I'm hearing. I warned her."

Sam cast a glance in her partner's direction. Bob's eyebrow hitched up.

She turned back to Gerald and asked, "Warned her about what?"

"About that ruddy career of hers getting her into trouble."

"Are you talking about anything in particular?"

"You name it, any topic under the sun that is illegal. She wants to be in line, the first one at the front of the chasing pack, to cover it. I blame her father for her insatiable appetite to get her hands on a story before any of her colleagues get a sniff at it."

"I don't remember her father, should I?" Sam asked.

"Yes, Donald Kilpatrick. He's a legend in the business. Unfortunately, he retired through ill health. He suffered a heart attack around ten years ago, when he was fifty-six. I suppose that was when Emily stepped up to the plate and took over from him, only on a smaller scale. Her father used to work for *The Guardian*. I believe Emily is trying to fill his shoes by going above and beyond for the local paper. I tried to warn her that being an investigative journalist for blokes is a totally different ball game for women, trying to emulate their counterparts, or in her case, her father. It's a pretty messed-up system if you ask me." He rubbed a hand around his face.

"Is that why you split up?"

"Yep. For what it's worth, I still love the blooming woman. I just can't live with her. It's hard to describe. It's as though she becomes obsessed when a story breaks or when the initial spark of interest emerges. Nothing else matters, including me and our marriage. What can I tell you? She's one determined young lady."

"Did you try to save your marriage?"

He launched himself off the desk and shouted, "What sort of question is that? Of course I did. Have you ever been involved with someone who has a desire to succeed running through their veins?"

Sam had to concede that she hadn't. "I haven't. Please accept my apologies. I didn't mean to cause any offence. Do you know what she's been working on lately? Before you answer that, we've just come from the paper's headquarters. Her colleagues didn't have a clue."

"Well, if they couldn't tell you, how the hell do you expect me to know? Of course, it depends on how recent you're talking about," he added, his anger subsiding a touch.

"That's as much as I can say. We're at a loss to know where to begin our investigation."

"Then I'm afraid I can't help you. She hasn't rung me in weeks."

"This is a long shot. Can you remember the names of any of her friends, in particular the ones she used to go out with?"

Gerald contemplated the question. "Not that I can recall, although she has been friends with Amy for years. I hope she makes a full recovery. She's always been a decent friend to Emily."

Sam removed a card from her jacket pocket. "If anything comes to mind after we leave, will you get in touch with me?"

"I will. I'm sure Emily will show up soon."

"I wish I had your faith. Thanks for speaking with us."

They left the unit, and before they got back in the car, Sam sighed and took in her surroundings.

"What's up?" Bob asked.

"Quite a lot, apparently. We've got one young lady lying in the ICU. Who knows if she's going to make it or not? And another one on the missing list, with no hint of what's happened to her. What if she's stuck her nose in where it wasn't wanted and someone has kidnapped her? Maybe they're torturing her as we speak."

"There you go again, letting that vivid imagination run away with you."

"I can't help it. In my defence, it only seems to really do it when there is a vulnerable woman at risk."

They entered the car.

Bob locked his seat belt in place and said, "Who says she's vulnerable? She's an investigative reporter. Since when did *vulnerable* and *reporter* go hand in hand?"

Sam started the engine. "Okay, that's a fair point." She suddenly thought of something she hadn't asked Gerald about and flew out of the car again. Opening the door to the unit, she startled the man who had resumed working on the motherboard. "Sorry, there's something else I forgot to ask."

With his hand over his chest, Gerald asked, "What's that, Inspector?"

"Could you give us your wife's address?"

"Sure, she still lives in the house we bought together when we were married. Forty-one Hamilton Drive. Stainburn."

"That's brilliant. Again, thank you for your help."

"You're welcome. I hope something comes of it. I'll keep trying to contact her in the meantime. Sorry, I should have said that before you left."

"Any help you or anyone else can give us at this stage will be gratefully received. Call me if you either see or hear anything."

"You have my word. I assure you, I'm as worried about her as you are, if not more. She was, and will always remain, my one true love."

Sam smiled. Totally understanding where his sentiment was coming from. "Don't give up hope. If she's out there, my experienced team and I will find her."

"That's good to know. Thank you."

She wandered back outside and inhaled a large breath before she got back in the car.

"What was that all about?" Bob asked.

"I forgot to get her address. There's no harm in us going around there to see what we can find."

"Whatever. To me, all it's going to prove to be is a waste of time, but you're the boss."

She pulled a face at him and drove off.

THE HOUSE WAS a semi-detached Victorian property with a small garden screened by a privet hedge at the front. Sam switched off the engine. "You stay here. I won't be a tick."

"If that's the way you want it."

"According to you, all this is a pathetic waste of time, so I wouldn't want to put you out, asking you to come with me."

He held a hand over his chest and groaned. "That one pierced the heart."

Sam smirked and tutted. "Whatever," she replied, mimicking him.

In the end, Bob joined her.

Sam knocked on the front door, as there was no doorbell in sight. It remained unanswered. There was a path off to the right that she suspected led to the back garden. "I'm going to have a look."

"I'll come with you, if that's permissible."

"Get you, spouting your long words."

He scowled but refused to respond to the dig.

The length of the garden surprised Sam when she opened the tall wooden gate. "Wow, this is huge. Furthermore, it's in good shape."

"Nice, very nice. I'm glad Abigail isn't here to see it. She'd be eager to have a garden this size, although it would be muggins here who'd be the one spending all his time cutting the lawn on his days off."

"But think of the pleasure it would give you, being able to hold barbecues for all your mates and not worry about what the kids were getting up to with a garden the size of a football pitch on their doorstep."

"Let's face it, men and women have very different ideas about what we'd do with a garden this size. All I'm seeing is a ton of back-breaking work."

"Enough of this debate. We'll have to agree to disagree, not for the first time lately."

"That's what men and women do, constantly. When I'm not disagreeing with you at work, I'm stuck at home with an unruly teenager and a wife who is always nagging me about putting the house on the market and taking the next step up the property ladder."

"Sorry, I didn't realise it was a sore point." Sam knocked on the back door and then tried the handle, only to find it locked. Her gaze was drawn to a large timber building halfway up the garden. It was much bigger than a shed, more like a summer house. She set off to investigate. It turned out to be the woman's office, which was unlocked even though there was plenty of computer equipment in there.

"Careless," Bob muttered behind her.

"I was thinking the same. I can't see her intentionally leaving this place unlocked, can you?"

Her partner shrugged. "I wouldn't, but who is to say what others prefer to do?"

"A missing woman and an unlocked office. It sends alarm bells ringing to me."

"Ordinarily, I would agree with you, except she went missing after a night out, not a day in her den or whatever you'd prefer to call this place."

"Admittedly, this place is immaculate, too. I doubt if my home office would be this tidy, if I was fortunate to have one."

"Hey, what are you up to in there?" a male voice shouted over the fence. "Get out of there, or I'm calling the police. You've got no right snooping around someone's garden when they're not at home."

Sam crossed the patio and produced her ID. "Sorry, sir. We are the police."

He strained his neck to check her warrant card. "Sorry, you can't be too careful these days. What do you want?"

"To speak with the homeowner. Do you know her?"

"Yes, go on, you tell me what her name is. You're not catching me out like that."

Sam smiled. "Emily Burke. Have you seen her lately?"

"Not since yesterday. We had a natter at teatime when she got home from work. I asked her if she wanted me to tidy up the front garden for her. I enjoy helping the neighbours out when I can, and sometimes she'll give me some vouchers to spend at the garden centre when she's able to get her hands on them. Freebies from working at the paper. Sorry, I tend to rattle on a bit. Why do you ask? Has something happened to her?"

"Possibly. From what we've found out so far, Emily met up with a few friends in town last night. One of them was run over, and no one has been able to contact Emily since. Several of her friends and colleagues have tried, but to no avail."

"Oh no. Well, I wasn't expecting you to say that. I noticed her car was missing last night. I thought she might have been called out to a story by her boss. It wouldn't be the first time she snuck out at night. She's eager to make an impression at that paper of hers, you know, to follow in her father's footsteps."

"So we've heard. What car does she drive?"

"A newish Renault. She doesn't know much about cars and asked me to tag along with her while she went shopping for one. The Renault was a bargain, and she's been chuffed with it ever since."

"So you're quite close to her, then?"

"Yes, and no. I'm not the type to take advantage if that's what you're asking. I do odd jobs for her here and there. It's my pleasure to help her out. I can only imagine what it's like to be a young lady on your own and trying to hold down an impressive job like she has."

"Does she confide in you?"

"We have the odd sit-down in the garden for a natter. I wouldn't necessarily say that she confides in me. I know she's still hurting from her marriage ending the way it did. She really loved Gerald. It's a damn shame because I think he loved her, too. Except he had trouble accepting her career and the dangers he perceived that came with it. In my opinion, they made a great couple. That's the trouble with people today. They're not prepared to stick with each other, even though they're still in love. Don't ask me why that is. In my day, you stuck with your partner through thick and thin. Life always throws the odd curveball our way when we least expect it. It's how we handle the bad times that really makes a marriage."

"That's so true. We've just spoken to Gerald, and he admitted that despite being divorced, he still loves Emily. I don't think I'm breaking any confidences there, from what you've just said."

"You're not. They're bloody idiots, the pair of them. They need their heads knocking together. Missing. I can't believe Emily is missing. Do you know how?"

"We're not sure right now. Our investigation is still in its infancy. The more we can find out about her and how she lives, the better."

"I reckon she was on to something dodgy. Sometimes I see the back bedroom light on until the early hours of the morning when I'm out here having a sneaky fag before going to bed. I know she uses that room upstairs during the winter when she works from home. She prefers the cosiness of the house, rather than freezing her bits off coming out here to her main office."

"Do you know if she's been in there lately?" Sam pointed at the timber shed.

"I think she was in there briefly yesterday. She came out carrying a handful of papers."

"It was unlocked with all her equipment inside, so that's a red flag to us."

"It would be to me, too. That's not like her, leaving that place unlocked. She must have had something important on her mind to forget to lock it."

"I don't suppose you have a key to the house, do you?"

"No. She wanted me to have one, but I declined. I'm funny like that. I'll do anything for anyone outside, but as far as any internal jobs that need doing, I'd rather do them when the homeowner is there with me. That way, they can't accuse you if things go missing or they mislay an item or two."

"Sounds like a good idea to me. It's better to be safe than sorry."

"I learnt my lesson the hard way. One of our neighbours along the road had a fall. I went down there to help, and the family ended up accusing me of taking money out of her purse. I swear I didn't. In the end, Barbara said she'd remembered paying the window cleaner twenty quid, the amount she thought was missing from her purse. She apologised to me for the mistake, but her son didn't. I told him to shove it and haven't set foot in her house since. I'm no thief, my heart is made of pure gold. I haven't got a nasty bone in this somewhat faltering body of mine. These days, it seems people are quick to jump to conclusions rather than realise when someone is trying to tell them the truth."

"I can tell you're a good man. Sorry you had to go through such an horrendous ordeal."

"Changed me for a while, I can tell you." He flung his hand in the air and said, "Stuff the lot of them, I thought. That was until I heard that Emily and Gerald were splitting up. Then my heart softened again. It was like a bolt out of the blue, came overnight, it did. She's such a lovely lady. Didn't deserve Gerald walking out on her the way he did."

"Maybe they'll realise what they had and get back together." Sam's mobile vibrated in her pocket. She removed it and said to the old man, "Sorry, I need to take this. Thanks for all your help. We'll go out the same way." She handed him a card. "If she shows up, will you call me?"

"Yes, I'll do it. I hope you find her soon."

Sam answered the call. "Sorry, Claire, I was talking to Emily Burke's neighbour. What do you have for me?"

"We've found a few items of note, ma'am. Do you want me to go over them with you now?"

"No, leave it until we return to base. We'll get on the road now."

"Fair enough. See you soon."

3

When they arrived, Sam was eager to see what the team had accomplished during their absence. Bob made them all a drink while Sam circulated the room. She stopped off at Claire's desk first.

"I've located a few of Amy's and Emily's friends, the ones they have in common. Rachel Wagner, Halima Callaghan and Penny Hunt. I'm in the process of sourcing their addresses and places of work."

"That's great news. I knew I could rely on you, Claire. Let me know what you find out, and Bob and I can get out there again, visit the women, see what they have to say about their evening out together."

"It shouldn't take long to find out the rest of the details, boss."

Sam moved around the room to see what Liam had for her. He launched himself out of his chair. "Where are you going?"

"Sorry, ma'am, I saw you heading my way and thought I'd switch the main TV on to show you what I've stumbled across."

"Carry on. Sounds intriguing." She stood closer to the TV. Bob joined her and handed her a mug of coffee. "It's movie time."

"If I'd known, I would have called in at the shop on the way back and bought some popcorn."

Sam flicked her hand at him, catching him on the arm. "Idiot."

The TV sparked into life, and Liam returned to his seat and tinkered with his keyboard.

"What are we watching here?" Sam asked. All she could see was a grainy picture of a road. By the look of it, the image was taken late at night. "Or am I being impatient?"

Liam smiled and pushed the clip forward a few seconds until two women came into view at the top of the screen. "I'm presuming these two women are Emily Burke and Amy Yokes."

"Blimey, they seem the worse for wear, or one of them does. She can barely stand upright; the other one is having to hold her up." Bob gave them an unnecessary running commentary of the events as they unfolded.

Sam dug him in the ribs. "Stating the obvious again."

"Sorry, did I say all that out loud?"

"Shut up and watch in silence."

Bob folded his arms and huffed out a breath. "Bloody charming, that is."

"As Bob has already stated, one woman seems worse off than the other one," Sam said, not taking her eyes off the screen.

"Maybe one of them doesn't drink alcohol," Suzanna suggested.

"Good point. There's no one else around. Where is this, Liam?"

"At the top end of Bridge Street."

"I'm with you. It's busier at the other end, near Tesco. So, the women were walking home? Why on earth didn't they take a cab?"

"Maybe they wanted to get some fresh air first," Claire chipped in.

"To help sober up," Sam agreed quietly. "It doesn't seem to have worked. Wait, what's this?"

Sam watched a car draw up beside the two women. The one who appeared to be sober bent down to speak with the driver. She opened the back door and helped the drunk woman into the back seat.

"What the fuck!" Sam said as she watched the driver take off before the other woman could get in beside her friend.

"That's not the end of it. Keep watching, boss."

Sam took a step closer to the screen. It proved to be too much for her eyes, and she stepped back again. The woman was standing in the middle of the road, gesticulating at the driver to stop. "Shit, is someone going to come along behind her and mow her down?"

No other cars appeared from behind the woman, but seconds later, the same car with the driver who had abducted the drunk woman came into view. The driver put his foot down, and his car clipped the woman. She spun and landed on the pavement.

Sam placed her hands on top of her head and shook it several times. "Oh, my fucking God, poor Amy. No wonder she's in a poor state in the hospital."

"Liam, we need to get the plates on that car," Bob ordered.

"Already done. The bad news is that the car was found down by the Derwent River this morning, burnt out. It was reported stolen last night, at around ten p.m."

"Jesus, so someone abducted Emily and tried to kill her friend. What type of animal are we searching for here? Liam, can you track the car for us, on the other cameras in the area, see what direction he takes and if, or should I say when, he swapped cars? He's not likely to take off without one, is he? It would only draw attention to him and Emily, especially if she was paralytic. Jesus, what a bloody mess. Those poor women."

"Can I add something, boss?" Claire asked.

Sam turned to face her. "Of course. What is it?"

"What if Emily wasn't drunk? What if her drink had been spiked, and this was a premeditated attack?"

Sam paced the floor in front of her team. "That seems the logical answer. Again, if Emily realised something like that was wrong with her, why didn't they opt to get a taxi home? That's all we're hearing about in the news lately, young girls and women getting their drinks spiked. Why aren't women taking better precautions instead of letting their guards down, if this is the result?"

"I don't think we should dwell on what has already happened, boss," Bob proposed.

Sam nodded and puffed out her cheeks. "You're right. Let's deal with what we know. Oliver, can you get onto the lab? We need them to go over that vehicle with the proverbial fine-tooth comb. We also need to send them a copy of this footage to see if the techs can enhance it for us."

"I'll get on it now, boss."

"Will someone get me the number of the chap whose car was stolen? I'll call him, see what he can tell us. There's a chance he might have seen it being stolen and can identify the thief."

"It's worth a shot. I can get that for you," Liam said.

"Claire, why don't you team up with Suzanna to sort through the information you need about the friends you've located? If nothing else, we need to ensure they're safe and weren't drugged as well, although I would have thought we'd have heard about it by now, if they had been. Jesus, I'm struggling to get my head around this. Two women's lives were gravely affected by a night out with their mates. And where the hell has this person taken Emily? Is this to do with a story she's covering, or is it down to something else entirely? We need to track her friends down. I think they'll hold the answers."

"What about Emily's parents?" Bob asked.

"Yep, I'm thinking we should contact them soon. If she's following in her father's footsteps, then there's a possibility they're very close. Maybe she confided in him about what she was working on. With Amy safe in the hospital, I think we should concentrate all our efforts on finding out what we can about Emily."

"It might be worth putting an officer outside the ICU, just in case," Suzanna suggested.

Sam's mind wandered to the last time they'd had to protect someone lying in a hospital bed. The victim had been none other than her fiancé, Rhys.

Bob nudged her arm with his elbow. "I could tell what you were thinking about. Are you all right?"

"I could do with a breather in my office. Can you oversee things out here for a few minutes?"

"Of course. Don't shut us out, we're all here for you, if you need us."

She touched his arm and smiled. "Thanks, Bob. You're a good man."

"That's debatable sometimes, according to you. Want a top-up?"

"Thanks, I'd love one."

"I'll bring it in."

Sam entered her office and stood by the open window for a few seconds. There was a definite chill in the air, but the breeze helped to clear her mind.

Bob deposited another mug of coffee on her desk and tentatively asked, "Do you want to chat about anything?"

"Shit, I said I would tell you in the car, didn't I?"

"I wasn't going to remind you. Shall I take a seat?"

"Yes. I'm sorry for being a grouch this morning. I have a lot on my mind."

"A problem shared and all that."

They both sat, and Sam flicked through the post vying for her attention as she contemplated telling her partner what was on her mind. Finally, she popped the letters in her in-tray. "It's Rhys."

"Doh, I guessed as much. What about him? Has he had a relapse?"

"No. He's been declared fit and got ready this morning, intending to go back to work today, but he froze. Had a mini meltdown in the hallway and couldn't leave the house."

"Oh heck, that's not good, especially considering his profession. How can he possibly help his clients or patients if he can't help himself?"

"I believe that same question was at the forefront of his mind and rendered him incapacitated. Er... maybe that's a bit of an exaggeration, but you get what I mean."

"I do. Hasn't he been in touch with a colleague while he's been recuperating?"

"Yes, Meredith was the one who announced he was fit to return to work."

Bob shrugged. "So, what's the solution?"

"I've told him to take another day off, go for a walk around the lake with the dogs. Hopefully, that will put right whatever is going on in that head of his. I have to admit to being concerned about him, though. He just needs to regain his self-confidence, that's what is lacking at present."

"It's bound to take its toll on him if he was stabbed outside his office. Perhaps he should consider moving his practice elsewhere."

"That's not a bad shout. I might run it past him later, time permitting. Maybe I should call him, and see how he's getting on."

Bob waved his hand from side to side. "Maybe give him a little while yet, catch up with him after lunch, after he's had time to chill on his walk."

"Yeah, I think you're right."

Liam knocked on the door and stuck his head into the room. "I've got the owner of the car on the phone, if you want a word with him, boss?"

"Brilliant. What's his name?"

"Ian Kenny."

"Do you want me to give you some privacy?" Bob rose from his seat.

"Thanks. I won't be too long."

She inhaled a couple of deep breaths to calm her nerves. It was one of her pet hates, talking to strangers over the phone. Given the choice, she'd much rather interview someone in person. "Hello, Mr Kenny. Thank you for agreeing to speak with me."

"You can call me Ian. I've told your colleagues everything I know."

"I'm sure. I'd just like to run through things again, if that's okay?"

"All right, but this is the last time."

"That's fine. Can you tell me when you realised your car was missing last night?"

"It was at around ten. I was closing the bedroom curtains, and I saw a man outside, near my car. I thought it was suspicious and opened the window to tell him to piss off. Sorry... He gave me the finger, opened the car door, jumped in and started the bloody engine.

The whole thing took less than thirty seconds, which is amazing, because some days it takes me more than that to get it started the normal way, you know, with a damn key."

"Did you get a good look at the man?"

"Not really. There are no streetlights near the house. Hang on, I've just had a thought."

"Oh, what's that?"

"I have a Ring doorbell. I'm not sure if it'll pick up the car on the drive or not but it might show the man as he would have passed the front door to get to the car, providing he didn't jump over the fence to avoid being seen."

"That's exciting. Would you mind checking and get back to me?"

"I'll do it now."

"Actually, if you give me your address, I'll send a member of my team around to see you. They can take a statement from you while they're there, if that's all right with you?"

"Not the best way to spend my day off, but yes, that's fine." He gave her his address, which she jotted down and then hung up.

Sam dashed out of the office. "Oliver, do you fancy a trip out to see Ian Kenny? He's going to check his doorbell camera footage, see if it picked up the person stealing his car."

Oliver pushed his chair back, and she handed him the address.

"You might as well take his statement down while you're there."

"I'll shoot over there now."

Oliver left the office. Sam glanced around the room. Everyone was busy with the tasks she'd set them except for one person, Alex. *Damn, I need to have a chat with him. I didn't mean to neglect him, it's just the day has got away from me a little.*

"Alex, can you join me in my office?"

He put down his pen and scraped back his chair, his expression unreadable, as normal.

Sam led the way into the office. "Take a seat. I'm sorry to hear your bad news. Bob told me about the bypass you need. Is there anything we can do to help?"

"Not really. I'm waiting to hear when the surgery will take place. It might be in a week, but it could be in a month. The consultant wasn't too sure, and then there're the doctors' strikes to consider."

"What will happen when you come out of the hospital?"

"You tell me, I haven't got the foggiest. There's no one at home to care for me."

"What about your friends or neighbours?"

"They'll no doubt go missing in action, knowing them. I'll be fine. There's no need to worry about me."

"We can rally around, take it in turns to come and stay with you for a few days."

"I wouldn't want to put you all out. You have enough to do around here as it is, boss."

"Leave it with me. I'm sure we'll be able to work something out between us. What about your kids?"

"They all live up in Scotland. I wouldn't want to impose on them."

"But you have told them you're ill and you need to have surgery, haven't you?"

His chin dropped to his chest. "I couldn't bring myself to tell them the truth. They've got their own lives to lead. They don't want to be bothered by their old man. I've had my time. I'd rather they got on with their own lives."

"Nonsense, you need to tell them… in case something goes wrong with the surgery."

His head rose. "I hadn't thought about that. I suppose I'd better get my financial affairs in order, just in case."

"Sorry, I didn't mean to… I think it's important that everyone has a will in place, especially in our line of work."

"I've been meaning to do it for ages. I'll get it sorted this week. Thanks for the kick up the backside, boss."

"When will you be leaving us?"

"I've got an appointment to see someone in HR this afternoon. I was going to mention it to you, ask for some time off, but then things got hectic around here and it slipped my mind. I didn't want you to think I was avoiding you by mentioning my predicament to Bob."

"The thought hadn't crossed my mind. We'll miss you when you go, Alex. I know we don't always agree on what techniques we should use, but I still regard you as a crucial part of the team."

"Thanks, that's great to hear. I know I can be a bit of a grouch. My two ex-wives can vouch for that."

Sam smiled. "Okay, let's see what HR have to say later and we'll discuss the matter again tomorrow. How's that sound to you?"

"Sounds good. Can I go?"

"By all means. I'll be out soon. I need to make a call first."

He left the room. Sam couldn't help feeling a tad guilty for the way she had treated him over the years. She tried to push that aside and rang Rhys. He answered on the fourth ring, sounding out of breath. "Sorry, have I caught you at the wrong time?"

"No, well actually, yes. I'm climbing a hill at the other end of Ennerdale, on my way back to the car."

"How wonderful, and how are you feeling?"

"I'm getting there. Bringing the boys out here has definitely helped put things back into perspective."

"There, see, I told you it would do you the world of good. Are you going to call in for lunch at The Gather?" She hoped he was going to say yes. Being around people would be another test he would need to conquer.

"I think so. I'll see how it goes. How's your day going?"

"From bad to worse, but that's another story. Don't ask. I'd better get on. Enjoy the rest of your walk. Give the dogs a kiss from me."

"Not likely. They're both soaking wet. They've had a blast romping about in the lake."

"Rather them than me at this time of year. Take care, love you."

"Love you, too. See you later."

Sam cleared some of her emails and opened a few letters, then called the hospital to check if there had been any change with Amy. Disappointingly, she was still the same. The nurse told her that Amy's boyfriend and parents were still at her bedside.

She relayed the news to the rest of the team and wandered around the room, gathering any information they had to offer. "How is it going, ladies?" she asked Claire and Suzanna.

"We're almost there. We should have the relevant details for you soon," Claire replied.

Sam moved around to her partner. "What have you been up to?"

"Chasing up a few ideas of my own."

Sam inclined her head. "Such as?"

"I've rung a few bar managers I know, asked them if they're aware of any spiking issues going on in their establishments lately. A couple of them said they've put notices up around the bar, warning people of the risks."

"I suppose that's a start. Have you rung the nightclubs in the area, too?"

"That was next on my list. How are you doing?"

"Better now I've spoken to Rhys. Sounds like he and the dogs have had a blast."

"And now you're jealous because you've been stuck at work, right?"

She grinned. "You know me so well, or think you do." She glanced over her shoulder and then leaned in to whisper, "And I had a word with Alex. See, I'm not as heartless as you think I am."

"Really?" He raised an eyebrow that earned him a jab in the stomach.

"You can be so cruel. I do my best with the team, considering what we have to contend with day in and day out."

"Things can always be improved. I thought you were the type of person who strived to be the best."

She took a swipe at his arm, but he dodged out of the way. "Cheeky sod." Sam dropped back to see how Claire and Suzanna were getting on. "Any news we can work with?"

"Yes, we've just this second finished." Claire handed her a sheet of paper with three names, addresses and workplaces written on it.

"This is great. We'll head out and have a chat with them. Come on, Bob, it's time to get on the road."

"Again," he muttered, then removed his jacket from the back of his chair and slipped it on.

4

Their first port of call was a building society in Whitehaven. Halima Callaghan was serving a queue of customers. She was the only cashier on duty when they arrived. They waited for the queue to die down, then approached the counter.

Sam held up her ID. "Hi Halima, is it possible for someone to take over from you so we can have a quiet word?"

"Umm... I suppose so. Let me check with my manager. Have I done something wrong?"

"Not in the slightest. There's no need for you to be alarmed."

"I'll be right back."

Luckily, no other customers came in while she was away seeking the permission needed to speak with them. Halima returned and said, "My boss is going to man the counter for me, we're short-staffed at the moment. One girl is on maternity leave and the other one is caring for her mother who is... sorry, you don't want to hear that nonsense. I'll let you through when Mr Jacobs arrives."

A man in his fifties gave them a cautious smile and shooed Halima out of the way. "Don't be too long. I'm expecting an important call from head office at three."

"We won't keep Halima too long," Sam assured him.

The door on their right clicked open, and Halima invited them in. "Mr Jacobs said we can use his office. What's this about? I can't think of a reason why the police should show up at my place of work, not unless something serious has happened. Oh God, it's not Mum, is it?"

Sam raised her hands to calm the young woman. "Please, it's nothing to do with your family, I promise. We're simply following up a line of enquiry about an incident that happened last night."

She frowned and invited them to take a seat in the small office. Halima sat in her manager's chair. "What incident?"

"First, I need to ask if you know Amy Yokes and Emily Burke."

"They're two of my best friends. Why?" Her gaze flitted between Sam and Bob. "God, now you're scaring me. Please, tell me what's going on."

"I'm sorry to have to inform you that Amy is in hospital. She's in ICU."

Halima slapped her hands to her cheeks. "What? Is this some kind of joke? This can't be happening."

"It's the truth. While we were at the hospital, her boyfriend told us she was out with friends last night. Were you with her?"

"Yes, there were five of us: Amy, Emily, Rachel, Penny and me. Do the others know? I have to ring them... tell them; they'll go berserk if I don't."

"Can we hold off telling the others for now? There are a few questions we need you to answer first."

"Gosh, okay, if I can. What do you want to know?"

"Where you went."

"We went to a couple of pubs, I think. My head is still a little fuzzy. Let's just say we had a good evening. But, what happened to Amy? You're not telling me it was the drink, are you? Wait, she wasn't that bad. She only had a few, compared to the rest of us. Well, Emily never goes over the top. She cares about her career too much to want to screw things up with her boss," she lowered her voice, so her boss didn't overhear her.

"Have you heard from any of your friends since last night?"

"No. Why won't you answer my question? How did Amy end up in the hospital?"

"We've since seen some very upsetting footage of the incident that took place last night. She was with another woman, who we believe to be Emily Burke. Emily looked as though she was drunk. A car pulled up alongside them. They might have thought it was a taxi. Amy helped Emily into the back seat, and the driver sped off. He turned the car around and deliberately ran Amy over."

"My God. Who was it? And where the hell is Emily?"

"We can't answer those questions. What we need to know is if anything happened to any of you during the evening."

"No, we were out having fun. No one bothered us or caused any trouble, if that's what you're asking, and Emily didn't have enough to drink to cause her to be legless."

"There's another possibility that we've come up with. That Emily's drink was spiked."

"Bloody hell, no. We're usually so careful with our drinks. We always watch out for each other." She covered her eyes with her shaking hand and sobbed. "I'm sorry. This is such a tragedy. Why? Why pick on us? On Emily? Do you know who took her? You must have seen him on the footage."

"It wasn't the best image, so was hard for us to determine who the person was. The driver remained in the car. During the evening, did anyone approach you at all? Start making a nuisance of themselves?"

"No, not that I can recall. It was a girly night out. We had a rule: no mentioning our other halves and, for the singles amongst us, no trying to pick up any men during the evening. We stuck to it as well."

"And you didn't spot anyone watching you?"

"No, but then I wasn't really looking. We take our personal safety seriously and would never leave our drinks unattended."

"You're sure about that? It seems to us that Emily might have been drugged, and you said yourself that she'd had significantly less to drink than the rest of you."

"I can't believe this has happened. Is Amy going to be okay? How hurt was she? Or is that a stupid question?"

"It's too early to tell. We haven't spoken with the doctor yet. All we can do is pray that she pulls through this."

Halima broke down again. "I've known her since we were eleven. We became friends on the first day of secondary school. There was talk of her and Russell getting engaged later this month. I hope that can still go ahead. They'd both be gutted if it didn't happen."

"I think it's a case of you all keeping her in your thoughts at this time. What can you tell me about Emily?"

"She's the strongest, most determined woman I know."

"That's the impression we've got from speaking with her colleagues. I don't suppose she told you what type of story she was working on, did she?"

"No, we tried to get it out of her at the start of the evening, but she refused to divulge what she was up to. We were all devastated because she leads the most exciting life out of the lot of us. We thrive on hearing what she's been up to. Do you think that's why this person has taken her? God, I hope she's not tortured or ra... I couldn't bear the thought of that happening to her, or to any of my other friends, come to that."

"That's why we need to find her, and quickly, before anything along those lines happens to her. Do you have any clue where we should start looking?"

"Me? How would I know? You're the police."

"I know, but we can't do our job properly without having input from people like you. We've been to her house and her place of work, even contacted her husband, but, as yet, we haven't come across anything we can class as useful."

"I'm sorry. I can't tell you anything else."

"Okay, then we'll have to leave it for now."

She rose from her chair to see them out. "I'm surprised you didn't get anywhere with her colleagues. I know Emily mentioned there has always been a lot of rivalry at the paper. Maybe that could have something to do with her going missing."

"We'll definitely delve into it."

Halima opened the security door and let them out, then she went back to relieve her manager.

"Thanks for all your help. Try not to worry too much about your friends."

"Easier said than done, eh? I'll drop by the hospital on my way home, see if Russell needs me to take him anything."

"Good idea. Give him a call first."

"I will. Thank you."

"I'm going to leave you my card, in case you think of anything after we leave that might help our investigation. Like I said before, we're at a loss to know where to begin with the enquiry, what with Amy unconscious and Emily missing."

"It must be tough."

"All in a day's work, we're hoping to fit Penny and Rachel in this afternoon, although time is getting on. We'll catch them at home later, if necessary."

Halima checked the time on her watch. "You might catch Rachel, if you're quick."

"The kids will be coming out of school now, so we'll drop by and see her. Thanks for the chat."

"My pleasure. I just wish I could have been of some use to your investigation. I'll keep my fingers crossed for Emily. I hope you can find out what happened to her soon."

"We're going to do our best."

THE SCHOOL WAS quiet when they arrived. Sam slammed the heel of her hand on the steering wheel. "Damn, I think we're too late."

Bob pointed at the main door. "Not necessarily."

Three women had left the building and were walking towards the parked cars over to their right.

"Quick, before they drive off."

They shot out of the car.

"Excuse me, ladies," Sam shouted. "Sorry to bother you. Do you have a moment?"

The three women stopped and glanced their way.

"Is something wrong?" the older woman asked.

"Not at all. We were hoping to have a chat with Rachel Wagner, if she's around?"

"I'm Rachel, and you are?" the blonde woman at the end asked.

Sam showed her warrant card. "DI Sam Cobbs, and this is my partner, DS Bob Jones. Would it be all right if we spoke to you in private? It's a personal matter."

"We've got to go anyway. We'll leave you to it, Rachel," the older woman said.

"Okay, see you tomorrow, girls."

The other two women left, their heads together in a whispered conversation.

"Do you mind telling me what this is about?" Rachel asked. "There's a bench over there. Shall we take a seat?"

"If that's what you'd prefer."

Bob removed his notebook from his pocket as they made their way over to the bench.

Once seated, Sam began the interview. "We've been told that you went out with some friends last night. Is that correct?"

"Yes, why do you ask?"

"I'm going to come straight out and tell you. Amy is in hospital, and we believe Emily has been abducted."

"What the fu...? Sorry, can you repeat that?"

"I think you heard. What we need to know is whether anything out of the ordinary happened while you were out last night."

"Such as?" The colour quickly drained from her cheeks. "My God, are you sure about this?"

"Yes, I realise this has come as a tremendous shock to you, but the more you can tell us, the more you'll be helping your friends."

"Don't you think I would if I could? I know nothing. All we did was go out for a drink. At the end of the evening, the three of us took a taxi while the other two, Amy and Emily, insisted on walking home. What happened to Amy that put her in the hospital? Please don't tell me someone attacked her."

"We have footage that shows Amy assisting Emily into the back of a car. The driver then drove off before Amy got the chance to get in herself. She was left gesticulating in the middle of the road. Moments later, the driver must have turned around because he came back into view and drove straight at her, sending her reeling."

Rachel gasped. "Oh my God, oh my God, oh my God! I didn't know. I haven't tried to contact them today. I assumed they had got home safely last night. I was going to give Emily a call later. Now you're telling me... what? That a stranger has kidnapped her?"

"So it would seem, yes. Which is why we felt the necessity to come and speak with you and your other friends. Perhaps you can tell me if anything out of the ordinary happened last night?"

"I'm trying to cast my mind back. Some of us consumed a fair amount of alcohol, which we rarely do, not on a school night. It was fun meeting up again because of our different commitments. It's been a while since we've been able to go out for a night on the town. Had it been the weekend, we probably would have ended up at a nightclub. What the hell is going on? Why would someone intentionally run Amy down like that?" Tears emerged, and her voice caught in her throat. "Oh God, more to the point, why would anyone want to kidnap Emily? Aren't women safe walking the streets at night any more? What are you doing about it? Apart from sitting here casually asking me questions about what we got up to last night. I can assure you, all we did was have a drink together and catch up with what's going on in our lives. And now you're telling me that two of my friends were attacked and you've got it on some kind of footage? None of this is making any sense. What are you doing to help my friends?" she repeated, her anger subsiding as the tears rolled down her cheeks.

"I know this is hard to hear. Please try not to get upset. Our investigation only started this morning. It might seem like we're not doing much, but I assure you that truly isn't the case. We have to ask what must appear to be inane questions to get to the truth. If you're telling me that nothing happened, then our job here is done, and that's when the frustration sets in for me and my team. With nothing concrete to go on, I'm afraid the case will grind to a halt quickly."

"But you have got something to go on, the footage. I'm sure that's more than most coppers have during an investigation."

"You're right, and we've done all we can to find the vehicle. We found it this morning. Turns out it had been stolen last night and whoever took it to use in the incident disposed of the car and set fire to it overnight. In the process, probably destroying any evidence there might have been in the vehicle."

"I'm sorry. I didn't mean to suggest you weren't doing your job properly."

"It's okay. We're used to getting flak from people who think all we do is drag our feet. The thing is, it's really important for us to do the groundwork for an enquiry, talk to the people who were last to see or be with the victims."

"I understand. It upsets me you're considering my friends as victims, but I get it. I wish I could tell you something, give you a clue that might lead to you arresting the bastard who is responsible. The truth is, there's nothing to tell."

"Okay, the one thing I haven't told you as yet is that we believe there's a chance that Emily might have been drugged. We're thinking someone might have intentionally spiked her drink."

"Oh shit, I never thought about that. It would explain the state she was in. Out of all of us, she's usually the one most likely to drink the rest of us under the table and be stone-cold sober. She was slurring her words last night. Being drugged would explain a lot."

"Why did Amy and Emily choose to walk home?"

"Emily was keen to clear her head. You know what, thinking about it, we thought she'd more than likely had a dodgy cocktail. We all had different drinks, which is why we thought we hadn't been affected. How would someone get the opportunity to spike her drink? Why her and not one of us lot?"

"It seems to us that she might have been specifically targeted. Could it have happened when someone went to the toilet? Did Emily take her drink with her and possibly leave it unattended while she used the facilities?"

"No, the drinks remained on the table at all times. We're usually so careful, watch each other's drinks like hawks. There are so many scare stories in the press these days. We made a pact to always watch out for one another. Are you telling me we let her down?"

"Not at all, but it would appear that her drink was spiked, if, as you say, there was no other reason behind her appearing to be intoxicated."

"Okay, but how will knowing this help Emily?"

"We're going to have to ask the pub where you went to check through their CCTV footage to see if it leads us to finding the culprit. Can you tell us which pub you visited?"

"The Horse and Hounds was one, and the other was The Globe. You're lucky it was only the two pubs we visited. Sometimes we go on a bender and visit five or six pubs in a night."

"Blimey, I guess we can count ourselves lucky then." Sam smiled, but Rachel didn't return it. Sam reached over and placed her hand over Rachel's. "Don't worry, we'll find her."

"Easier said than done on both counts. I doubt if I'll sleep tonight. I hope you find Emily, and soon, before anything truly bad happens to her. Christ, all we did was go on a night out together and, if this is the result, we're going to think twice about doing it in the future. I heard a worrying statistic on the radio yesterday."

"What was that?" Sam queried.

"That violence against women is at its highest. There are over three thousand complaints made by women to the police every single day. If that's true, what hope is there for the future? How has it come to this? Equality, my arse; we might think we've got it, but have we really? My God, we're effing entitled to it, but women are still classed as the weaker sex, aren't we?"

Sam closed her eyes for the briefest of moments and sighed. "It's hard to admit it, however, I fear you're right. We should be able to walk the streets alone without the need to dread what will happen to us if we do. The statistics don't lie, it's disheartening to hear and we're trying to do our best to bring those figures down daily."

"And failing by the sound of it. The person on the radio also said that the attacks on women last year far exceeded those of terrorism in this country. It beggars belief."

"It is what it is. As a force, we're doing our very best to combat the issue, and if it wasn't for the government insisting on cutbacks, I think there would be a good chance of us getting a handle on things and bringing down those stats."

"I realise your hands are tied, but you're not instilling any confidence in me that you'll find Emily anytime soon."

"We've made it our priority. That's all I can tell you at this stage. There's no way we'll be giving up on Emily, I promise you. Don't lose faith in me and my team."

"I won't. I'm sorry if that's the way it came across."

"It didn't, not really."

"I have a tendency to speak what's on my mind when I'm angry, no offence intended. Where do you go from here?"

"We'll put a call out to the two pubs, get them to view the footage for us and call round to see your other friend, Penny, see what she can add. Are you sure you didn't see anyone hanging around last night, making a nuisance of themselves?"

"No, not at all. I would've told you." She shook her head and appeared to be deep in thought. "You don't suppose this has anything to do with Emily's job, do you? She told us last night that she was closing in on a new story."

"Closing in? Did she say what it was?"

"No, frustratingly, she can be a bit of a tease when she wants to be. Have you contacted the paper she works for? They'll probably be able to tell you."

"We have. Her colleagues were as much in the dark about what she was working on as you."

"That's terrible. I've warned her several times in the past not to be so secretive about her stories. She once told me that was half the thrill of it. She could be a little warped, as well as determined. You know her father used to be one of the best investigative journalists around, don't you?"

"So we've heard. So, what you're saying is that she tries to exceed her father's achievements?"

"I suppose so, or at least match them. She's always been the same. That's why her marriage failed. Gerald had finally reached the end of his tether with her because once she got her teeth into a project, there was no going back for her."

"Had that sort of tenacity got her in trouble in the past?"

"Occasionally, with her boss. I'm telling you this as her friend. She's got no fear. Maybe that's why the person who abducted her drugged her, because they knew they wouldn't be able to get their hands on her any other way."

Sam nodded her agreement. "That seems logical. Are you sure she hasn't dropped a hint along the way?"

"No, I would tell you if I knew. I'd do anything to help rescue my friend."

"I'm sure you would. Okay, then we'll leave it there for now. I'm going to give you one of my cards. Ring me day or night if you think of anything else I should know."

"I will. I hope for all our sakes you find her soon."

"Are you going to be okay to drive home? We could drop you off on the way, if you're not up to it."

"No, I'll be fine. I don't live that far away. Actually, I might even walk home. It'll help to clear my head, which is still a little muzzy after last night. It'll also give me a chance to have a think on the way. Please, promise me you won't give up on her. I hear of so many cases in the media reporting that a body has been found months after the police have closed an investigation."

"No case is ever closed until it has been solved. I promise, my team is all over this. Don't worry. It was nice to meet you. I want to reassure you yet again that we're going to do our very best to bring Emily home safely."

They all rose from the bench.

Sam shook Rachel's hand. "Take care of yourself."

"Thank you. Good luck with the investigation."

Sam and Bob returned to the car. Inside, Sam tipped her head back and watched Rachel walk over to her car, retrieve her jacket, then lock the vehicle again.

"She seemed really cut up about her friend," Bob said unnecessarily.

"Wouldn't you be? You do say the weirdest things at times, partner."

"Pardon me for breathing. I was only saying..."

"Well, don't. All you're doing is stating the obvious. We need to head over to the beauty salon now to see if Penny has any clue about what's going on."

"It'll probably be much of the same. The two women we've spoken to so far have told us exactly the same, in a roundabout way."

"I know, but she might have spotted someone lurking, you never know. Which is why it's imperative that we question everyone who was with Amy and Emily on their night out."

"I get that. I was just throwing my tuppence worth in."

"I know. Sorry for having a go at you. Let's pay Penny a visit, then I suggest we should call it a night."

"Sounds perfect to me."

Penny was locking up the beauty salon when they arrived. "Sorry, I'm closed. You'll have to come back tomorrow."

Sam smiled and flashed her warrant card at the woman through the closed door. Penny opened it immediately. She was petite and dressed in a bubble-gum-pink overall, with the name *Penny* embroidered on the top pocket. "Sorry to trouble you so late in the day. Do you have time to spare for a brief chat?"

"It'll have to be quick because I'm supposed to be meeting my boyfriend at five-thirty. He's taking me out for dinner." She glanced down at her uniform. "It may not be the perfect outfit for a date, but I can't miss the chance of him paying for dinner. It doesn't crop up that often. Sorry, I'm wittering on as usual. What can I do for you? Oh heck, don't tell me the neighbours have put in another complaint about the noise of the extraction fan, have they? I had it serviced last week, and it doesn't appear to have made a blind bit of difference. I had every intention of calling the company again today, but it's been too hectic around here. I even skipped lunch to squeeze in one of my regulars."

Sam held up a hand to stop the woman from talking. "Honestly, our visit has nothing to do with any extraction fan. Can we come in?"

"Sorry, yes, please do. May I ask what this is about, then?"

"We're dealing with a new enquiry, and your name has cropped up."

"What? I haven't done anything illegal, and if someone has told you I have, then they're bloody lying."

"Sorry, it's been a long day. Let me clarify things for you."

They all took a seat, and then Sam went through what had happened to Amy and Emily. As expected, Penny had the same reaction to the news that Rachel and Halima had.

"Wow! Jesus, do you know who has taken Emily?" Penny asked, clearly gobsmacked.

"Not at this time. The car she was picked up in was later found burnt out. That would have been a key piece of evidence if the driver hadn't resorted to such drastic measures to cover their tracks. We don't want to hold you up too long. Can you tell us if you saw anything you thought was suspicious last night?"

"No, not that I can recall. We were all having a relaxing time. Maybe we're guilty of letting our hair and our guard down at the same time. I kept nagging the girls about getting a taxi with us, but they pooh-poohed it and told us that Emily needed to get some fresh air. I wondered if she was sickening for something. She was acting really strange. The thought never occurred to me, or the others apparently, that she might have been drugged. Bugger, thinking back now, we should have realised there was something wrong. Why didn't we listen to our instincts?"

"I don't mean this disrespectfully, you were probably compromised by the alcohol you had consumed during the evening."

"I think you're right. That's not an excuse, though. We agreed to watch out for each other, to prevent our drinks from getting spiked. I can't believe someone would stoop so low and that Emily was the target. Do you think this has something to do with her job? She's had a couple of threats in the past because of the stories she's covered. I call her my fearless heroine."

"What type of threats? Do you know who made them?"

"She waved them away, wasn't concerned about the bastards at all because they've all since been banged up in prison."

"Interesting. We'll go back to the paper and see what they have to say about this."

She sucked the air between her teeth. "I doubt if they will help you. She was keen to keep that type of thing close to her chest."

"May I ask why?"

"In case her father found out. He's got a couple of friends who moved up from London and work on the paper. I'm sure they keep him updated with what's going on in her life, if only professionally."

"Ah, I understand. Do her parents live locally?"

"Yes, close to Emily. I'm sorry, no idea of their address, but it shouldn't be hard for you to track them down, should it?"

"We'd like to think not."

"Can I visit Amy? Do they allow visitors to the ICU?"

"I think they do. My advice would be for you to leave it for a few days, maybe ring the ward, see how she's doing, although they probably won't reveal her status to you. Are you in touch with her parents or her boyfriend, Russell?"

"Not really. I'll chance my luck in a few days. Maybe I'll send her some flowers."

"Again, not every ward allows flowers, so it might be worth you checking before you spend out."

"Gosh, I never thought about that. I'm sorry, I'm going to need to get a move on. Frank will be waiting for me. He hasn't got a lot of patience, bless him, he's likely to storm off in a huff if I'm late. That sounded awful, saying it out loud. I didn't mean he's got a problem."

"Don't worry. I think we've covered everything now. I'll give you one of my cards."

"I'll have a think during the evening and get back to you."

"If you wouldn't mind, thanks."

She let them out of the shop and locked the door behind them.

"She seemed to have her head screwed on, concerned about the boyfriend, though," Bob said on the way back to the car.

"What are you saying? That you wouldn't be ticked off if Abigail kept you waiting at a venue after work?"

"Honestly, no. Mind you, I'm pretty confident that she would never do that, only because she likes her food too much."

Sam bit her lip to prevent herself from laughing and got in the car. "I'm not sure how to respond to that."

"What have I said now?" he asked innocently.

"I'll let you think about that while I drive back to the station."

The car remained silent for the next few minutes. "Damn, yeah, it wasn't the best choice of words, was it? Don't tell her, for God's sake, otherwise she'll take pleasure in snipping my nuts off and serving them to me, passing them off as meatballs in a sticky barbecue sauce."

Sam laughed until tears ran down her face.

"All right, calm down, it wasn't that bloody funny."

"Wasn't it? I think it's going to be a while before I can rid myself of that image. You are such a comedian, without even realising it."

"Gee, thanks. I'm glad I've brightened your day."

"Oh, you have, don't worry about that."

He crossed his arms and grunted, "Glad to be of service, considering how your day started out this morning."

"Thanks. It's gone from one end of the spectrum to the other."

He muttered something indecipherable under his breath and stared out of the side window.

Sam chuckled inside. It's so damn easy to wind you up, my friend. You have a habit of falling for it, hook, line and sinker, every time.

5

He waited until darkness descended, ensuring that the woman was alone. He'd watched her come home on foot about thirty minutes ago. He'd been surprised to see her walking at first but, upon reflection, it only really shocked him she'd driven the car to work that morning at all, after what she had consumed the night before. He would have been legless after one cocktail. It wasn't his type of drink, especially if it was a mixture of spirits. Mind you, he was a 'beer and nothing else will do' kind of chap, anyway.

From his viewing point, by the shed in the back garden, he saw the bathroom light go on. Music began playing inside the house, which made him smile. *Happy to hear that; it will deaden any noise I might make getting in there. She's so thoughtful, without even realising it.* His shoulders jiggled as he laughed.

He left it another five minutes and then made his move. He'd already planned how he was going to get in. The kitchen window was open slightly, which would suit his purpose, but he still tried the back door in case she'd left it open in her haste to have a soak. The disappointment of finding the door locked soured his mood. He cast an eye around the garden. His gaze fell on a wooden crate stacked on top of a pile of stones at the bottom. When he picked it up, he considered it sturdy enough to hold his weight. He placed it under the window and tested it, just in case his assumption was wrong. Happy to continue, he checked his position, ensuring the neighbours wouldn't see him, and then climbed through the open window.

Beneath him, the draining board was empty. He dropped to the floor and removed his shoes to deaden any noise he might make on the tiles. Overhead, he heard the music and Rachel singing along to it. Eager to get on with things, he weaved his way through the living room and crept up the staircase to the first floor. Peeking through the spindles, he could tell which room was the bathroom. It was the first one at the top. He continued on his journey and stood outside the bathroom door, listening. The pause gave him time to work out the rest of his plan. All the time, he was conscious of the fact that Rachel was married and her husband could be back any second.

He pulled on his mask and began counting down, something he often did before making an important move in his life. Three, two, one! Casually, he entered the bathroom. Rachel was lying in the bath, her eyes closed, apparently mesmerised by the charismatic voice of Michael Bublé. He stood there for a second or two, admiring how beautiful she was, despite the mound of bubbles spoiling his view.

He laughed, startling Rachel.

Her hands automatically tried to cover her modesty. "What the fuck! Who the hell are you? What the hell are you doing in my house? Get out of here immediately or I'm going to call the police."

"Get out." He picked up the green bath sheet she'd placed on the toilet seat and threw it at her. She caught it, preventing it from hitting the water.

"No. I won't do it. You can't make me."

He took one step towards her, clenched his fist into a tight ball and connected with her jaw. The blow knocked her out cold, and she slipped under the water. He tutted, rescued the towel and pulled her out.

"Oh, dear, did you get your hair wet?" Laughing, he yanked her to her feet, held her upright and inspected every divine inch of her. "I haven't got time to do what I want to you, here, but I'm prepared to wait." Ham-fistedly, he wrapped the towel around her body then hoisted her over his shoulder. He paused at the top of the stairs to make sure the coast was clear for him to leave. She was lighter than he thought she was going to be, despite her height. After collecting his shoes from the kitchen, he used a tea towel from the long handle in front of the oven to open the back door. He left the door ajar and made his way to the car which he'd parked in the back lane. The vehicle was stolen, so he wasn't that concerned if a neighbour spotted it and reported it to the police once the news got out.

I've thought of everything, well, mostly. It'll be the only time I slip up. The police have no idea who I am or why I'm abducting the girls, but that's okay, as long as I know, that's all that matters.

He chuckled and shoved Rachel into the back of the car. The house was only a few miles away. There was no chance of her waking up en route. At least he hoped there wasn't.

At the other end, he checked his surroundings before he removed his hostage from the car. He eased her over his shoulder and ran up the path to the front door. Key in hand, he opened the door and closed it quickly behind him. He searched his pocket to find the key to the cellar and unlocked that door next. The light turned on automatically as he took his first step. In the cellar, he deposited the woman in the room next to Emily's. She was talking, but he couldn't make out what she was saying because of the soundproofing he'd installed. He grinned, pleased that his plan was coming together with no hiccups. From the corner of the room he collected the clothes he had purchased from the charity shop and tipped them onto the bed. Then he finished drying Rachel with the towel and dressed her in the velour leisure suit. It was tight in places and turned out to be too short in the leg. *Tough, it'll have to do.*

Rachel stirred. Her eyes flickered open and widened when she saw him smiling down at her.

"Please, what's this all about? Where am I?" she asked, her voice quaking with fear.

"All will become clear when the time is right. There's really no need for you to be worried. All your friends will be here soon, and then the games will begin."

"What games?" She scrambled across the firm camp bed and hunched up against the stone wall. "What are you going to do with us? You won't get away with this."

He cocked an eyebrow and smiled at her. "Won't I? We'll have to see about that, won't we? If you're a good girl, I might go easier on you than the others. Just remember that... when the time comes."

"Comes for what? What are you talking about?"

"Patience, dear woman. Patience. I know most people don't possess it these days. I'm asking you to dig deep. It'll be worth it in the end, I promise." He backed up towards the door.

"No, wait. You can't leave me here like this."

"Ah, you're wrong. I can do what I like with you and the other prisoner because I have the power at my fingertips, unlike either of you. Now rest, you're going to need to conserve all your strength for what I have in mind."

He closed the door with enough force to emphasise his point and ran up the stairs. He locked the door and returned to the car. After driving a couple of miles up the road, he waited until the traffic died down and set the car on fire. It exploded as he ran to take cover in the middle of a nearby cluster of trees. A thrill surged through him that brought a sinister smile to his face. Two down, another two to grab. *It was unfortunate about Amy, but maybe she'll make a full recovery, and I can try to add her to the collection at the end.*

Once he was certain the car had been destroyed, he set off on foot, enjoying the peace and stillness the night air offered during his trip. That was until the sirens spoilt things. He upped his pace and returned to the safety of his parents' home. There, he knocked up an omelette large enough for three. He devoured his meal first, not caring if his prisoners' food got cold by the time they received it. *They should be grateful I'm feeding them at all.* It had been a mixed bag in the past, with the other girls he'd abducted. His plan had developed somewhat since then. He hadn't kept the other girls at the house, they'd been secured in a locked room at a warehouse that was due to be demolished. Unfortunately, he wasn't aware that the demolition date had been brought forward. He watched on in terror as the building was razed to the ground before his eyes. The two girls' remains had been found a few days later, and the entire area had been cordoned off and regarded as a crime scene.

He'd visited the site, along with dozens of inquisitive onlookers, finding it exhilarating to linger that close to a crime scene. He made a note of how the police went about their business. It had proved an eye-opener to him, so much so that it had got his juices flowing enough to formulate another plan, which was now approaching fruition.

The two women rejected the food he gave them, although they had accepted the glass of water that was on offer. He checked the buckets in the corner of the room. Neither of them had used the facilities. "Don't forget, it's wrong of you to hold on; use the buckets as they're intended. You're going to be here for a while."

He'd laughed, left the cellar, cleared up the kitchen, and then settled down in front of the TV with his pad, noting down his objectives for the following day. He intended to make the most of his week off from work. He had no plans of going away, not at this time of the year. Why should he bother when he had the house to himself and there was no chance of his parents returning?

He made a few notes, detailing what he would do every hour of the day. He needed to get on the road early, aware of what the next woman's daily regime looked like. Exhausted, he fell asleep and woke up to the music of *News at Ten*. After giving the living room a quick tidy and checking the kitchen was in order, he made his way upstairs to bed. As soon as his head hit the pillow, he was back in the land of Nod, as if he didn't have a care in the world.

HIS ALARM WENT off at five-thirty. Without showering, he slipped on his jeans and jumper and left the house. With another car in mind, he walked up the footpath onto the next estate and took his chance. The car was one of the easiest he'd got into. He drove off and arrived at his destination with a couple of minutes to spare. With his adrenaline pumping and his heart racing, he observed the woman's house. The light went off in the front bedroom. He hunkered down in his seat, in case the woman came out of the house and came his way instead of taking her usual route of jogging through the woods, a few streets away.

Right on time, Halima left her house and jogged through the estate, over the patch of green between several of the bungalows, and made her way off the estate. He followed her at a steady crawl, not wishing to alert her to the fact that he was behind her. When it was clear that she was going towards her usual location, he put his foot down on the accelerator and pulled up slightly ahead of her.

There was a lack of houses in this part of the estate, therefore, he didn't feel he was taking a risk getting out of the car, wearing his mask. Halima had wires coming from her ears, listening to her music the old-fashioned way. Totally focused on her run, she hadn't noticed him until he stepped in front of her. She opened her mouth to scream, but he slammed a fist into her stomach. Halima doubled over, and then he gave her an uppercut, which knocked her out. She was slightly chunkier than the others. Maybe that's why she was out here every morning for a run. He bundled her into the back seat of the Corsa he'd chosen. It was a tight squeeze, but the journey wouldn't take them long.

At the other end, he carried out his usual routine of checking his surroundings first. However, this time, because of the extra weight Halima was carrying, he had to drag her to the front door, causing his anxiety to spike. *I need to make it quick before someone sees me. Damn, she weighs a ton compared to the others; fat-shaming comment, but it's the truth, so I don't give a shit!*

He heaved her through the door and down the stairs to the cellar and threw her on the camp bed in the third room. The woman stirred.

"Welcome to your new home, Halima. I hope you're going to be happy here." He grinned, but she couldn't see it behind the mask he was wearing.

"What? Who are you? Why have you kidnapped me? What are your intentions?"

He wagged a finger. "Oh my, you are an inquisitive one, aren't you? You just sit there, or lie if you prefer, for a while, and things will become obvious shortly."

Halima shot off the bed and ran towards the door. He quickly blocked her path and punched her in the stomach, winding her. She creased up, staggered backwards and fell onto the bed.

"There, now that was silly, very silly indeed. You're going to pay for that when the time comes."

"Let me go. Please, I'm begging you. I'm claustrophobic. I'll go out of my mind if you leave me here alone."

He applauded. "Wonderful, that's going to add to the drama. What about the dark? I suppose you fear that, too, do you?"

"Yes, yes, please, you can't leave me here alone. I'll die."

"Not too soon, I hope," were his last words before he left the room.

Before he exited the cellar, he listened outside the three doors. Silence, except for the odd sob here and there. It meant that all his efforts at making the cellar soundproof hadn't worked and it instantly soured his mood. He locked the cellar, went through to the kitchen and made himself a bacon sandwich to console himself. He checked the cupboards and found an unopened packet of cereals he could give to the women later. It was that or nothing, so it would be up to them if they ate it or not.

6

Sam arrived at work at around eight-fifty. After they'd had dinner with Doreen the previous evening, she and Rhys had chilled out, just talking. At the end of their chat, he admitted he wasn't ready to return to work yet, which was fine with her. She was keen to reassure him that there was no rush for him to force himself back to his practice. He'd been through an horrendous ordeal, and even though it was his job to mend other people's minds, he needed to be fully recuperated himself before he could heal others. She advised him to keep doing what he was doing, getting out there in the open air, visiting different places and exercising the dogs. He confessed he was worried about putting their neighbour out. Sam had assured him that Doreen wouldn't mind. As long as she spent a few hours here and there with Sonny, she'd be more than willing to fit in with their plans.

It was Rhys' well-being and recovery that was paramount to all of them. He had finally conceded that she was right and thanked her for being so understanding. In truth, money was tight, but she had no intention of telling him how tight it was, fearing it might cause a setback in his recovery. She had a couple of thousand stashed away in an ISA that she could withdraw from if things got too bad.

"Hey, are you all right?" Bob snuck up behind her.

"Damn, why do you always do that to me?"

"Er... it wasn't intentional. I'll just come in and sit at my desk in the future, until you notice me."

"Now you're being ridiculous."

"You started it."

"I'll be in my office. Let me know when the others arrive, if you would?"

"I might do," he called after her.

She entered her office and slammed the door. Her mood worsened when she saw the amount of paperwork stacked in a neat pile on her desk. "Jesus, you're having a bloody laugh." Rather than gripe about the task that lay ahead of her, she sat, determined to make a dent in it before the rest of the team showed up.

She opened her second brown envelope of the day and was interrupted by the phone. "DI Sam Cobbs. How may I help?"

"It's Nick on the front desk, ma'am. Do you have a moment? I'd like to run something past you."

"Of course. In person or over the phone, Nick?"

"In person would be preferable. The thing is, I'm the only one on duty down here."

"I'm on my way." She knew it must be important. Nick wasn't the type to waste her time. She passed through the outer office, shouted a quick hello to the team who were there and ran downstairs without giving them an explanation of where she was going. No doubt she'd get the third degree from Bob upon her return. "Nick, what's up?"

"Thanks for coming down, ma'am. I was going through the incident reports which came in overnight, and two in particular caught my eye." He turned his clipboard around to face her.

Sam read the two incidents he had highlighted with a yellow marker pen. They were both referring to burnt-out vehicles. "How strange. Could it be a coincidence?"

"I'm not sure what the likelihood of that could be. I just thought you should know."

"Okay, my team is snowed under at the moment. Can you chase

the reports up for me? Send a couple of your men around to see the owners of the vehicles. I'm presuming the cars will have been stolen. No one's likely to set fire to their own car, are they?"

"I'll get on it, ma'am. I just wanted you to be aware."

"Will you let me know how your men get on? Get them to ask the homeowners if they have Ring doorbells. They seem to be all the rage at this time. If they have, try to get the footage and we can compare it to what we have from the incident that has already come to our attention."

"Leave it with me. I'll see what I can do."

Sam smiled and patted his hand. "Thanks, Nick. You were right to bring this to my attention."

He winked at her. "I'm rarely wrong."

Sam smiled. "You should be a permanent member of my team."

He sniggered. "Umm... and then I would miss dealing with things like this, not to mention the abuse I receive from the public from time to time."

"Well, if you ever change your mind, let me know." She peered over her shoulder to check there was no one around who could overhear them, then whispered, "I've just heard that I might be losing a member of my team."

Nick's eyebrows shot up. "That's unfortunate. Can I ask who?"

"Alex. Don't go saying anything to him. He's been told he needs a heart bypass. I can't see him returning to work after he's had an operation of that nature, can you?"

"Blimey, I didn't know he was ill. That's a big deal and, yes, I think you're right. It could take months for him to fully recover from such a procedure."

"We're waiting on what HR has to say about it. In the meantime, have a think about what I said."

"I thought you were joking. I'll definitely have a serious think about it, ma'am. Thank you for considering me."

She turned towards the security pad and punched in her number, then grinned at him. "It's a case of better the devil you know, Nick."

They both laughed. Sam ascended the stairs to report the news to the rest of the team.

"Bugger, what does that mean, exactly?" Bob was the first to ask.

Sam shrugged. "Could be one of two things. Either it's kids having a laugh copying what they've seen on TV, or my other suggestion would be that the two incidents are connected to the case we're already working on. As we're under pressure, dealing with what's already happened to Amy and trying to find Emily, I've asked Nick to look into it and report back to me if his men find out anything of interest."

"Makes sense," Bob agreed. "What do you want us to do?"

Sam did a quick head count. Everyone was there except for Alex. "No sign of Alex yet?"

"No. I've tried calling him, and there's no answer," Oliver said.

"That's not good. Oliver, if we haven't heard from him in thirty minutes, will you go round to see him, just to make sure everything is all right?"

"Okay, boss."

Sam went over what she expected from the team for the rest of the day and then carried her coffee back to the office. She had plans of her own to attend to, like calling Fearne at the newspaper. She blew on her drink, took a sip, then dialled the number and asked to be put through to Fearne. Unfortunately, she couldn't give the receptionist the young woman's surname.

"No worries, I believe I know who you're referring to. Let me put you through now. If it's the wrong person, I'll get her to pass you back to me and we'll try again."

"Much appreciated, thanks."

"Hello, Fearne, speaking. Is that you, Inspector Cobbs?"

"Ah, there you are. Sorry, I forgot to take your full name when we met. Do you have time for a quick chat?"

"I do. It's quite slow around here today. Famous last words, eh?"

"Nothing like tempting fate to turn your day on its head. Okay, I'll come straight to the point. We met up with some of Emily's friends yesterday. They told us they had been with Emily the night before.

Five of them went out to a couple of pubs in town. None of them were aware of what had happened to either Emily or their other friend, Amy, who ended up in hospital. Sorry, I'm waffling on when I said I would get to the point, which is, her friends are concerned that her abduction might be the result of a story that she was working on, or possibly one that she'd covered in the recent past."

"The same thought has been running through my mind during the night. I've barely slept a wink."

"Has anything come to mind?"

"No, nothing. We're as much in the dark about what she was working on, I swear."

"You mentioned before that she's very secretive at work. Is that acceptable, or is she usually one for bending or breaking the rules?"

"The latter. Emily drives our boss nuts, but then, when her stories finally emerge and highlight something major happening in the community, he tends to forgive her. She's generally given free rein to do what she likes after cracking that paedophile ring at the nursery. She showed a bucket-load of guts and determination to bring that one to print."

"I understand, which brings me back to what her friend Penny said."

"Oh, what's that?"

"She said that Emily had received some threats in the last few months."

"Wow, really? That's news to me."

"Damn, I was hoping she might have confided in you."

"Sorry to disappoint you. Emily prefers to go it alone, that's what makes her so unique and better than the rest of the journalists around here," she lowered her voice and whispered the final part of her sentence.

"Okay, that's me hitting another brick wall, then. I was hoping you might give us a lead or two. I don't suppose you'd be willing to share the last couple of stories she was involved in, would you?"

"Sure. I can't see any harm in it."

Sam picked up her pen and jotted down the information that

Fearne located once she'd logged in to her computer. The main one being the paedophile ring case. "I can't thank you enough, Fearne."

"You're more than welcome, but if anyone asks, I wasn't the one who gave you the information."

Sam smiled. "I hear you. You've got my card. If ever you need my help in the future, don't hesitate to contact me."

"That would be amazing. I swear not to bother you too much."

Sam cringed, hoping she hadn't made a mistake, offering an ear or shoulder to cry on for the enthusiastic young journalist. "Thanks again for all your help. Have a good day."

"You're welcome. I'll be keeping my fingers crossed you find Emily soon."

Sam ended the call and rested her head back to mull over what she'd been told by Fearne. Is it worth checking out? Throwing our resources into something that might turn out to be a useless line of enquiry? There's no doubting that Emily was the one who was specifically targeted on the girls' night out, so it would be remiss of us not to chase it up. So, why is my gut telling me otherwise? What's that all about?

She left her office and stopped off at Claire's desk and shared the information she had received from the young journalist. "Can you do some digging if you're not too busy, Claire? See how the land lies. Compile a list of those involved and their whereabouts since then. Check if there are any members of the ring who are still out there, on the run."

"I've got the gist, boss."

"If you need a hand, ask Suzanna to join you."

"If there are two of us on the job, we'll get a result quicker."

"Done. Suzanna, can you help Claire, please? She'll go over everything with you."

Suzanna nodded and moved her chair closer to Claire's desk.

Sam rested a hand on her shoulder. "Thanks."

"Where do we go from here?" Bob asked.

"We've still got a few loose ends to tie up. Maybe we should delve into Gerald Burke's background, see if there are any negatives there for us to follow up on."

"You reckon the husband has got her somewhere? I'm confused. Everyone we spoke to yesterday, including him, told us he still loved her and if it wasn't for her job, they'd probably still be together."

"Humour me," Sam said and wound her way back into the office to complete her paperwork, or at least see how far she could get before she was interrupted again.

Oliver poked his head around the door about twenty minutes later. "All right if I head over to Alex's now, boss?"

"Still no sign of him?"

"No. What's worrying me is that his phone is diverting to voicemail straight away."

"Go, let me know what happens."

Oliver left the office. Sam sat there and reflected on her relationship with Alex over the past few years. She couldn't say she didn't like the man, but there was something about him that hadn't clicked with her over the years. She had never taken him to one side and had a chat with him about his life outside of the station, unlike she had with the rest of her team. Maybe that had something to do with her distancing herself from him.

She caught herself reading the same email over and over and tapping her pen until Oliver rang her. "Oliver, what's the news?"

"Not good, boss. I looked through his front window and saw him lying on the floor. I called an ambulance right away and then broke a window to gain access."

"Shit. Where are you now?"

"The ambulance is on its way. I'm trying my best to wake him."

"You're going to dig deep for your CPR training."

"I've never had to do it, not on a real person but... shit, okay, I'll have a go."

"I'm going to send Liam over to give you some support. Hang in there." She ended the call and shot out of her chair. "Liam, get over to Alex's. Oliver could do with a hand. There's no telling how long an ambulance is going to be."

"Shit! I'm on my way." Liam took off like a greyhound out of the traps.

Sam rested her backside on a nearby desk and placed her hands on her cheeks.

"Are you all right?" Bob asked from his desk. "Can I get you a drink?"

"A glass of water, thanks, Bob. I hope he's going to be all right."

"So do I," Bob admitted as he handed her a paper cup.

Claire and Suzanna looked equally worried as they got back to the task at hand.

"Bloody hell, how has it come to this? Why didn't any of us know what was going on with him? He needed us, and we've all let him down."

"Hey, you can't say that. He's always kept his personal life to himself. How were we to know that he was that bad?" her partner said, trying his best to reassure her.

"Bob's right, boss. None of us were aware, otherwise we would have kept a closer eye on him," Claire said.

"Thank God Oliver went over there, I dread to think what…"

"Don't go there. Let's see what the paramedics say first, before we let our minds wander into unknown territory."

Sam nodded. Bob was right. What was the point in them worrying about what might have been and how they could have combatted it?

Her phone rang in the office. She ran to answer it on the third ring. "DI Sam Cobbs."

"It's Oliver, boss. Just to give you an update. The paramedics have worked wonders. He's awake and on his way to the hospital."

Sam sighed and collapsed into her chair. "Thank God for that. Is Liam with you?"

"He's just arrived. Do you want me to go with Alex to the hospital?"

"Yes, you do that. Tell Liam to come back to the station. I'll check Alex's file for his next of kin and get in touch with them."

"Roger that."

Sam pulled up Alex's personnel file on her computer. Nigel, his eldest son, was listed as his next of kin. Sam rang the number on the screen.

Nigel answered the call after several rings. "Hello?"

"Hi, Nigel. Sorry to trouble you. I'm DI Sam Cobbs, your father's boss."

"Oh shit! Has he been hurt in the line of duty?"

"No, although he is on his way to the hospital."

"What? Why?"

"It's his heart. Can you come and be with him?"

"Damn, I can't. I'm in the middle of a course. If I drop out, I'll have to retake it next year."

"I understand. What about one of your siblings?"

"Leave it with me. I'll reach out to them via our WhatsApp group. Which hospital?"

"I'm assuming they'll be taking him to Whitehaven. Saying that, if he needs surgery, he might be moved to Newcastle."

"Bugger. Okay, we're all up in Scotland. I'll have a chat with the others. Someone will be there soon, I promise."

"Much appreciated. I'll keep in touch with the hospital in the meantime."

"Thanks for letting us know. He's always spoken fondly about you, Inspector."

Sam closed her eyes as another imaginary dagger pierced her heart. "I think a lot about him, too. He's a good man," she felt the need to say.

"He's a grouch most of the time, but he's got a heart of gold."

"I'd better let you go. Nice speaking to you, Nigel."

"You, too. Thanks again for getting in touch."

Sam put the phone back in its docking station and covered her face with her hands. That's how Bob found her a few seconds later.

"Hey, nothing's happened to Alex, has it?"

"No. I've just got off the phone with his son. He can't make it, but he's going to speak with his siblings. He assured me that one of them would make the trip down to be with Alex."

"That's great news, although he'll be livid."

"Then he's a bloody idiot. He should have made them aware of his heart condition. And another thing, I feel so damn guilty."

"What are you talking about? You couldn't have known this was going to happen. He only told us about his heart yesterday."

"I know. It was something his son said."

Bob shrugged. "Which was?"

"That Alex always spoke fondly about me to his family."

Bob chewed on his lip and then started laughing.

"What the fuck is wrong with you?" she demanded, infuriated that he should find the situation amusing.

"I bet that made your day," he said, tears filling his eyes as he doubled over with laughter.

She slapped him. "You bastard. I knew I shouldn't have told you."

"I'm sorry. Your face is a picture, though. Guilt, it's such a futile emotion, especially if it has no foundation."

"Screw you. Here I am, spilling my guts out, and you're standing there taking the piss out of me. How can you possibly call yourself a friend?"

His face twisted into a grimace, and he tutted. "Get over it. Boss or not, you do talk a lot of twaddle at times."

Sam went to slap him again, but he dodged her hand.

"You've got to be quicker than that."

"I'll bide my time and catch you when you're least expecting it."

Their banter was interrupted by the phone ringing again. Sam gulped down the lump that swiftly appeared in her throat to answer it, fearing that she was about to receive yet more bad news about Alex. "DI Sam Cobbs. How may I help?"

"Sorry to trouble you again, ma'am. I wondered if you had a spare minute to come down and talk with a concerned member of the public."

"All right, Nick, I'm on my way." She didn't bother asking what it was about, putting her trust in the desk sergeant's judgement. She replaced the phone and told Bob, "I won't be long. I'm needed downstairs."

"Want me to join you?"

"You might as well bring that notebook of yours, just in case."

They left the main office and made their way down to the reception area to find a man in his mid-thirties waiting for them.

"What is it, Nick?"

"This man is Tom Wagner. He's just reported his wife missing, ma'am."

Confused, Sam's brow wrinkled.

Bob elbowed her and whispered, "Rachel Wagner."

"Oh my God. Yes, of course. I'm so sorry. Is there an interview room free, Sergeant?" she asked, her mind, along with her heart, racing.

"Room One is available. Shall I bring you all a drink?"

"Not for me," Tom replied.

Sam shook her head. "We're fine. Thanks."

"Speak for yourself," Bob grumbled beside her.

"This way, Mr Wagner."

"Call me Tom. Is this going to take long? I'd rather be out there searching for her than be stuck in the police station for hours on end."

"We shouldn't be too long." Sam led the way down the narrow corridor. She opened the door and invited the anxious man to take a seat.

Once they were seated at the table, Sam asked, "Perhaps you can tell us what makes you think your wife is missing?"

"Because she wasn't at home last night and she wasn't there when I woke up this morning."

"And I take it that's unusual for your wife?"

"Definitely. She never goes out without telling me. There's something else I need to tell you. Her car is missing."

"Okay, well, I might know the answer to that."

"What? Why would you know? What's been going on? And why has my wife been leaving me in the dark?" He thumped his fist on the table, making Sam and Bob jump.

"If you wouldn't mind calming down, it's all quite innocent."

"Tell me!" he demanded a second time.

"I will, if you give me the chance. We went to the school yesterday to interview your wife..."

"About?" he shrieked.

"I'm not going to continue this conversation unless you can control your anger. I've already told you that our visit was quite innocent."

"I apologise. You've got to understand how worried I am. This is so unlike her."

"I completely understand, but you getting angry won't help find your wife, will it?"

"Sorry, please forgive me."

Sam smiled, showing there were no hard feelings. "There's nothing to forgive. You're obviously extremely worried about your wife. Have you tried calling her? I assume she has a mobile."

"She has, that's just it. I found it on the side in the kitchen. She never goes anywhere without it. Sorry, why did you go to the school? I need to know."

"We wanted to ask her a few questions about her night out with her friends."

He frowned and shook his head as if to clear his mind. "None of this is making any sense. Please, can you tell me what you discussed with my wife? What does going out with her friends have to do with anything? It's hardly a rarity. They're always going out together. Admittedly, not so much lately as they've all had a lot of other commitments to focus on."

"We're investigating a couple of very disturbing incidents involving two of her friends."

"Care to enlighten me? Rachel hasn't told me about any of this."

"The night before last, the evening your wife and her friends went into town, Amy was involved in a hit-and-run, and the driver abducted Emily in that same vehicle."

"What the... are you sure? Why wouldn't Rachel tell me something as important as this?"

"I don't know. In your wife's defence, when we spoke to her at school, she admitted she was still suffering from a fuzzy head. That's why she left her car at work. We actually interviewed her later on in the day, as she and a couple of her colleagues were making their way out to their vehicles."

"So she walked home. Is that what you're telling me?"

"Yes, she told us she needed to clear her head after we informed her of what had happened to Emily and Amy."

"Jesus Christ! Why didn't she tell me?"

"Well, your wife obviously made it home last night. May I ask where you were?"

"I was working late. I have a couple of major projects that need to be completed by Christmas."

"What do you do for a living?" Sam asked as Bob jotted down what Tom was telling them.

"I'm in engineering, a designer. I build boat engines for a company in Whitehaven, although I'm classed as self-employed. Don't ask, it's too complicated to explain."

"I won't because it sounds it. What time did you get home?"

"Gone eleven."

"And when did you notice your wife was missing?"

"Not until this morning. We've got an arrangement; my wife is a light sleeper, so I always kip in the spare room if I'm home later than ten as she often goes to bed early, especially after she's been out on the pop the night before."

That excuse sounded plausible to Sam, given how bad Rachel said she was feeling when they'd interviewed her. "What do you think has happened to her?"

"I don't bloody know. If I knew that, I'd be able to find her, wouldn't I?"

"Have you called her parents? Gone through her friends' list to find out if anyone has seen her?"

"No." He placed an iPhone on the table. "That's her phone. I've tried to figure out what the passcode is, but I can't open it."

"Can we let our tech guys try?"

"Please do. That's why I brought it with me, hoping you would suggest doing just that. I'm really worried about her."

"I know. Just a few more questions, and then we'll get this over to the lab. Was her bed slept in?"

His hand covered his eyes, and he gasped. "Oh shit, now you mention it, no, it wasn't. Does that mean she went missing during the evening?"

"Possibly. When was the last time you spoke with her?"

He dropped his hand to look at Sam. "Yesterday, at breakfast. She was in the kitchen, popping a couple of paracetamol for the bad head she was nursing." He fell silent and then chewed on his lip.

"Have you remembered something?"

He closed his eyes and let out a sigh. "The bath was full, and the floor was wet."

An imaginary hand clutched her heart. "Right, we're going to need to send a forensic team out to see what they make of the scene."

"Oh no. What do you think has happened to her?"

"It sounds to me, just on the information you've given us, that maybe an intruder has got into your house and abducted your wife."

"No, Jesus, I can't bear to believe something like that has happened."

"What about the cars?" Bob muttered beside her.

"What did you say? Are you accusing me of doing this?" Tom shouted. He stood and tipped back his chair.

"He wasn't insinuating anything of the sort. Please, Tom, sit down. Let's discuss this like adults."

"I refuse to until he has the courage to say what he said again, louder this time, so we can both hear."

Bob shrugged. "All I said was, what about the cars?"

Tom righted his chair and threw himself into it. "What are you talking about? Is that some kind of code between the two of you?"

Sam could have killed Bob for opening his mouth. She nudged him with her knee under the table.

"Sorry," he apologised. "I shouldn't have said anything. Something came to our attention earlier that may have a connection to the case we're working on."

"And?" Tom said, still frowning, because Bob's explanation lacked any useful information.

"The person who put Amy in hospital and who abducted Emily ditched the car later that night. It was found burnt out."

"I repeat, what does that have to do with Rachel going missing?"

"First thing this morning, we were informed that two more cars had been found burnt out overnight. It's possible that one of them might have been used by the person who has abducted your wife. Of course, that's pure conjecture on our part at this stage, with no solid evidence to hand."

"But you don't believe in coincidences and can see a pattern developing, is that it?"

Sam nodded. "We would be neglecting our duty if we didn't give the facts any credence."

"So, where do we go from here? What are you going to do about finding my wife? I take it you haven't found the person responsible for kidnapping Emily and putting Amy in hospital, yet?"

"No, we haven't. Our investigation is ongoing. We're sifting through the evidence we have and still making enquiries on that front."

"And now my wife has gone missing..." His voice trailed off, and he coughed to clear his throat. "Damn, the thought of her being in the clutches of a madman is... indescribable. Please, you have to help me. This person can't be allowed to get away with this. What's the point of having CCTV cameras dotted around the town when you don't use them?"

"Who said we aren't using them? It's thanks to the cameras that we witnessed what had happened to Emily and Amy. However, I feel the need to add that the incident occurred in town, so the likelihood of it being caught on camera would have been a lot higher. Do you know if there are any cameras close to your house?"

"No, I can't think of any?"

"Do you have a Ring doorbell camera?"

"I can't stand them, feel they're an intrusion. Rachel kept bugging me about getting one, but I refused to bow to the pressure. Some of our friends have got them. They think they're great, but I've yet to be convinced."

Shrugging, Sam said, "It's another way of proving what's taken place. The owner of the car involved in the incident with Amy and Emily could show us the footage from his camera. It showed the man stealing his car."

"Really? That's amazing, so you know who this guy is, then? What's stopping you from picking him up and arresting him?"

"Because he was canny and disguised himself. Therefore, we couldn't identify him properly."

He bounced back in his chair and raised his hands. "There you go then. I rest my case. If the cameras are there to show the criminals attacking someone's property or car and the criminals see fit to disguise themselves, then what's the frigging point in spending out a fortune on the equipment in the first place? That's been my argument all along, the cost of the damn things. Sorry, we've drifted off track now."

"I understand your point of view entirely, however, sometimes the equipment has its merits and comes up trumps in certain crimes. Do any of your neighbours have the systems installed?"

His gaze dropped to the table, and he twisted his wedding ring. "I can't think of anyone. That's not to say they haven't got them. I can knock on a few doors when I get home, find out for you."

"That would be very helpful, thank you."

"Is there anything else you need from me?"

"I think we've covered everything now, unless you can think of anything else you want to add? No, wait, do you have any idea how this person entered your home?"

He slapped his hand against his forehead several times. "Shit, shit, shit, I should have realised…"

"Realised what?"

"When I came down this morning, the back door was open. It must have been open all night. I went straight to bed when I got in, didn't go near the kitchen in case I woke Rachel. It's all adding up now, isn't it?

Whoever took my wife must have taken her out the back way. There's an alley behind the house. It's pretty dark out there, no streetlights. The locals are always complaining to the council about it. Maybe this person was aware of the fact, perhaps they had stalked my wife, followed her home and... oh, I don't know. I'm at a loss about what to think about this. It's messing with my damn head. Why the fuck didn't I check the back door before I went to bed, or even check that Rachel was okay in bed last night? I feel guilty about my reckless behaviour."

"There's no need for you to feel guilty. If you're telling us you work late regularly and you and your wife sleep separately occasionally, then why on earth should you feel guilty?"

He sighed and shook his head. "I suppose I'm searching for a reason to blame myself for not being home last night. If I hadn't worked late, Rachel might be safe right now. She's not. Instead, she's another statistic on the missing list. Tell me, how many missing people remain on that list, Inspector? I want the truth."

"I can't give you an exact figure. All you need to know is that my team and I are the best this station, and Force, has to offer in this county."

"That's reassuring, thank you." He rose from his seat. "I need to go. I have an important meeting I have to attend at eleven and I've yet to make any notes to prepare for it."

Sam raised an eyebrow and stood. "I understand. Thanks for dropping in to see us, to report your wife missing. Umm... we're going to need access to your property, or should I say Forensics is. If you're going to be busy at your meeting..."

"There's a spare key under the flowerpot by the front door. They can use that."

The fact that Tom wasn't prepared to postpone his meeting for a day or two sent alarm bells ringing for Sam. Nevertheless, she smiled at him. "Very well. We'll see you back to the main entrance. Here's one of my cards. Don't hesitate to get in touch with me if you think of anything else we should know."

He took the card and followed her out of the room to the reception area, where he shook her hand. "Thank you for seeing me and, more importantly, for taking me seriously."

"You're welcome. I'll keep in touch. You'll be the first to know when we find her."

"I'm glad you said *when* and not *if*. I'm praying that's the case. It's worrying that the same person might kidnap or abduct, whatever you prefer to call it, both Rachel and Emily. I should have asked you before. Do you know why Emily was taken?"

"We don't. As you know, she's an investigative journalist. We're looking into the recent cases she's reported on, to see if anything suspicious comes to light."

"Gosh, I never even thought about that. Fair enough in Emily's case, if it has something to do with her career, but that doesn't explain why the same person should come after my wife, does it?"

"That's the dilemma we're facing. You're right, there's no rhyme or reason to it. There's something I should have covered with you, as well, before we say farewell. Has Rachel mentioned lately if anyone had approached her? Threatened her? Anything along those lines?"

He shook his head. "Nothing that I can recall. Can I think about it and get back to you later today?"

"Of course you can."

He left the station, and Sam and Bob returned to the incident room. Bob made them both a drink while Sam explained the situation about Rachel to the rest of the team.

It was Claire who suggested something that Sam should have really thought about herself. "Does this mean that someone is setting out to kidnap the group of friends who went out that night?"

Sam slapped a hand to her brow and pinched at it, massaging her temple as the first signs of a headache emerged. "Shit, we need to contact the others, make sure they're safe."

Claire and Suzanna each picked up a phone and dialled the numbers Claire had written on the notepad alongside her.

"No answer from Halima," Claire said.

Everyone's gaze went to Suzanna, who closed her eyes and grimaced. "Same here. Penny isn't answering her mobile, either."

"All right, let's not panic. Can you try the women's places of work, please?"

Claire was the first to report back. "Shit. Her boss is livid because Halima hasn't shown up for work and she hasn't rung in sick, either."

Sam punched her thigh. Two cars burnt out overnight. Rachel's disappearance could explain one, while Halima's abduction might account for the other. What the fuck is going on here?

"Hi, Penny. Thanks for taking my call. I have DI Cobbs here. She'd like a word with you." Suzanna took it upon herself to pass the phone over to Sam, which Sam appreciated as she was eager to speak to the woman in person.

"Sorry to disturb you, Penny. I know how busy you are, so I'll make this quick."

"It's okay. I don't have a customer booked in for another half an hour. What can I do for you, Inspector?"

"Have you heard from Rachel or Halima lately?"

"Shit, no, I was supposed to call them last night, but I had an emergency to deal with when I got home."

"Oh, sorry to hear that. Nothing too bad, I hope."

"My cat got run over. I spent hours at the vet's with her."

"How awful. Is she all right?"

"We're not sure if she's going to pull through yet. I'll know later. She's my baby. If anything happens to her…"

"So sorry you're having to deal with this on top of everything else. I'll keep my fingers crossed for you."

"Thank you. Wait, why are you asking about Rachel and Halima? Bugger, don't tell me something has happened to them."

"Sorry to have to tell you that Rachel's husband, Tom, has just left the station after reporting Rachel missing."

"What the fuck… what the hell is going on? Is she missing or has she been kidnapped, like Emily?"

"We're presuming the latter. Our first instinct was to check if you and Halima are all right."

"I'm fine, apart from freaking out about my cat. Shit, what about Halima?"

Sam expelled a large breath. "Sorry to have to tell you that her boss informed us she hasn't shown up for work and we're unable to reach her on her mobile, either."

"What the... Jesus, how? Why would someone kidnap them?"

"We tried calling your mobile but didn't get a response. We were worried about you, hence the reason we've called the salon."

"I'm fine. I think I've left my mobile at home. I was so distraught about my cat... fuck, you don't think she was run over on purpose, do you?"

"I wouldn't like to say. Do you know who did it? Did anyone witness the accident? Any of your neighbours?"

"It was late last night. I heard a squeal of tyres, and my first thought was with Kitty, my cat. I ran outside and found her lying on the road. She was bleeding, looking up at me with her beautiful green eyes, pleading with me to help her." Penny sniffled. "Oh, no, I can't stop crying. She's such a sweetheart. I only let her out about fifteen minutes before while I got her dinner ready. I was about to call her in when I heard the commotion going on outside."

"I hope she's going to be okay. Right, I know this is probably the last thing you want to hear right now, but there's a possibility that the same person who has Emily has abducted both Rachel and Halima."

She paused and sobbed. "What? No way! What does this mean? That I'm next? That someone is going to—"

"Okay, keep calm. Hear me out. I'm going to ensure that doesn't happen. Can you lock the door to your shop?"

Penny sighed deeply. "I can't. I have customers arriving any minute."

"That's fine. I'm concerned about your safety, no one else's. You can open the door when you see your customers arrive. Do it now, Penny, while I'm on the phone."

"Bloody hell. I'm so scared."

Sam listened as Penny walked towards the door, then the sound of the bell ringing made Sam catch her breath. Penny screamed, and Sam dropped the phone on the desk. "Keep the line open, Claire. Bob, Liam, Oliver, come with me. Now."

. . .

Bob drove to Whitehaven. It took them almost fifteen minutes to get there. The door to the salon was wide open, and there was a crowd of people standing outside the premises. The four of them shot out of the car.

Sam produced her ID. "What's going on? Where's Penny? Has anyone seen her?"

A woman in her early forties stepped forward. "I saw a man pull up outside the shop. He knocked Penny out and carried her over his shoulder towards his car. I was dealing with a customer in my shop, and we both ran outside. We tried to stand in his way. He was too strong for us, pushed us both to the ground and drove off."

"Are you both all right?"

"Yes, no actual harm done."

"Can you describe him?"

"No, he had a hoodie on that covered his face. I'm sorry, we tried to help Penny. I rang the police; they told me someone was already on their way. How did you know she was in danger?"

"I was on the phone with her when the bastard struck. She was about to lock the front door. We suspected someone was on the way to abduct her."

"Holy crap. That poor girl. I wish we could have done more to help her. The truth is, we didn't stand a chance."

"Don't go blaming yourself. Do you know if there are any cameras in the vicinity?" Sam glanced up at the shop frontage. There were none on view outside the salon or the lady's shop next door.

"I don't have them, but Ernie over the road has only just had them installed."

"Which shop? The hardware store?"

"Yes, that's the one. What shall we do about Penny's salon? I can't keep an eye on it. I have my own customers to attend to."

"Don't worry, leave it to us." Sam turned to the rest of her team. "Liam, can you call the station? Get a patrol team out here. Also, put in a call for SOCO to attend. I think it's going to be a waste of time, but it's still something we need to put in place. Oliver, can you get the crowd back? Ask if anyone saw the incident, get a statement from them and tell the rest to move on."

Both men nodded and went about their duties.

"Bob, we should see what Ernie can show us, if his cameras are working properly." Sam held up her crossed fingers.

"Let's hope so."

They marched across the road. An elderly man, who must have been well into his seventies, opened the door for them. He wore a khaki-coloured overall, and his spectacles were sitting on the very tip of his nose.

"Hello, sir. Are you Ernie?"

"That's right. Did Coleen tell you? I saw you speaking to her."

"She did. She told us you've recently installed security cameras here. Is that right?"

"Yes. I have, that's correct. Oh, I see why you're here now. Yes, come out back. Let's see if the cameras picked up anything."

"Did you see the incident?"

"Yes, I was dealing with a customer. He told me what was going on because I had my back to the window. We were both shocked as the events unfolded. I'm sorry to say that we're both in our seventies. We thought it best to stay out of it. Had we been twenty years younger, we would have tackled the bastard. I know that's not much help for you."

"Don't worry. There are other ways you can help us. Hopefully, your cameras will have caught the suspect."

"Yes, yes, I do hope so. We'll soon find out. The question is whether I'll be able to work the damn thing."

"I can have a look at it for you," Bob was quick to volunteer.

"Would you? That would be marvellous. I'm terrible with technology. My daughter and son-in-law persuaded me to have the system fitted. There have been a lot of break-ins lately, and the shoplifting incidents are going through the roof. That was even highlighted on the news the other day. It's got to stop, otherwise shops like mine will go out of business. What will punters do then? Keep shopping online, no doubt; it's killed the high street. Look around you at the number of shops boarded up in this part of the town. Shocking, it is. Sorry, you don't want to hear all my woes."

"Don't worry, we're all aware of the damage that has been caused to this town in recent years. It's utterly devastating, but I'm not sure anyone has the answer to the problem except for the men in suits in the House of Commons."

"Ain't that the truth? And they don't care. They don't live in the real world, they can't do, can they? As long as the capital, London, is thriving, that's all that matters to the likes of that mob."

Bob took a moment to get himself accustomed to the equipment. "Right, here's hoping I've worked this out properly. Don't go criticising me if I cock up."

"I've got the instruction manual around here somewhere." Ernie checked the shelf alongside the equipment.

"I doubt if my partner will take any notice of it, Ernie, so I wouldn't put myself out if I were you."

"That's right, put me down in front of a stranger. I'll just hit this button here and prove you wrong, shall I?"

He did just that, and Sam grinned at him. "There, I knew with the right encouragement, my hero here would come up trumps."

Ernie tipped his head back, laughed, and then punched Bob lightly on the top of the arm. "I reckon she knows you better than you think she does, lad."

Sam sniggered, and Bob grunted something indecipherable. Then the three of them concentrated on the small screen and watched a man pull up. His car was parked at an angle to the kerb, and he had his hoodie up. He sprinted up the couple of steps to Penny's salon. Seconds later, he exited the property with the young woman thrown over his shoulder.

"Shit, it happened as Coleen told us. Penny didn't stand a chance," Sam whispered. "The car, can you focus on that, see if we can get a numberplate from it?"

"What's the point?" Bob asked, "we know it'll more than likely end up being stolen."

Sam sighed and blew out a breath. "If you have a better suggestion, I'd love to hear it."

Out of the corner of her eye, Sam could see Ernie's head shifting from side to side as the banter rifled between her and Bob. She suppressed another giggle at the man's amused expression.

"Don't mind us, this is typical," Sam told him.

"My wife and I used to have the same kind of petty relationship before she slipped away from me through cancer."

Sam touched his arm gently. "I'm sorry to hear that. How long ago?"

"Three years now. There's not a day goes by when I don't think about her. I get caught out now and again, making two mugs of coffee or plating up for two our favourite meals. I suppose it'll get easier in time."

"It's so hard saying goodbye to our loved ones. My heart goes out to you."

"Thank you. I really wasn't looking for any sympathy. Back to business. You're probably going to ask me for a copy for evidence, aren't you?"

"I can do it for you. It's no problem," Bob volunteered. He selected another disc from the packet of one hundred sitting on the shelf and began the process.

Ernie cringed and gestured with his head in Bob's direction. "I bet you're glad you brought him with you."

"He has his uses, now and again," she leaned in to whisper. "Not that often, and I wouldn't tell him, either. His head is big enough as it is."

Bob tutted and let out a guttural growl. "I am here, you know, listening to all this rubbish."

Sam pinched his cheek. "You know I'd be lost without you, partner."

"Yeah, right? Okay, it's all done. Thanks for trusting me, Ernie. I've kept the original disc in there, so you can keep recording for the rest of the day. That way, you won't mess up your system if you have one."

"I have, thank you, young man. Here, take one of those plastic cases. You might drop it, and then where would you be?"

"You're too kind. Thanks for all your help, Ernie."

"My pleasure, as always, to help the police."

Ernie saw them to the front door and shook both of their hands. "I hope the evidence helps nail the bastard for what he's done today. Any idea who he is or why he's abducted Penny?"

"I wish we knew. The clues are few and far between right now. Penny isn't the only kidnapping case we're dealing with at the moment. Two, maybe three, of her friends have also been kidnapped."

"What? Oh my Lord, I didn't know. What a shocking thing to happen, and you're still none the wiser about who's behind it all?"

"Nope. Not a clue. We're hoping that the more evidence we gather, the more it will help us. Again, thanks so much for all your help. Take care of yourself."

"I will. I'm so glad my daughter and her husband persuaded me to fit the equipment now."

"So are we. I think it's going to be a tremendous help."

Sam and Bob crossed the street to join the rest of the team. By then, Oliver and Liam had successfully encouraged the crowd to move on. "I'm going to check on Coleen, make sure she's okay." She entered the grocery shop next door to the salon. "How are you, Coleen?"

"I made us both a mug of coffee to calm our nerves. We're all right now, aren't we, Jan?"

"We are, but what about that poor girl? What are you going to do about her?" Jan asked, incensed.

"We're going to do our very best to get the word out about her. I have to ask, Coleen, have you seen anyone hanging around the salon lately acting suspiciously?"

"Now why on earth would I be looking out for someone like that? I can't say I have, not really. We've got a bus stop not twenty feet away from us, so make of that what you will."

Sam sighed. "Oh well, it was worth a shot. I'll get a member of my team to take a statement from you before they leave, if that's all right?"

"It is. I'm willing to do anything I can to help Penny. Did you get what you were after from Ernie?"

"Yes, he caught it all on camera. We've made a copy of the footage. Right, I'd better get on with the investigation. I'll leave you one of my cards, should anything else come to mind."

"Yes, that's a good idea. I'll ring you if it does. Please, don't dilly-dally during your investigation. Penny is a lovely girl." Tears filled Coleen's eyes. "I dread to think what's going to happen to her."

"Try not to dwell on it too much. We're going to do all we can to find them all."

"What? Who? What are you saying?" Jan was quick to ask.

Sam rubbed her hands over her face. "We believe that overnight, two more of her friends have been abducted. That's as well as the friend who was abducted a couple of nights ago. That's not all. Another of Penny's friends is currently in the ICU after the suspect mowed her down with the car he had stolen."

"My oh my. I didn't know. You just don't hear about things like this going on, do you? Well, I sincerely hope you find them all and can do it quickly, before something unthinkable happens to them. Do you know why the girls have been targeted by this fiend?"

"We're struggling as nothing has come to our attention as yet. We're hoping to speak with the girls' families during the day. Hopefully, one of them will shed some light on why."

"I don't envy you at all," Jan said and took a sip of her drink.

"I sense we have a tough day, or couple of days, ahead of us. I must get on, ladies. Thanks for your help. Stay safe."

"I've got a German shepherd at home called Lucas. I might go home and fetch him, for added security."

"I'm sure the suspect won't return. I truly believe he's targeted these women for a reason. We just have to work out what that reason is and where he's likely to be holding them."

"What about the car he used?" Coleen suggested. "Didn't you see his numberplate on the footage from across the road?"

"The trouble is, going by the other vehicles he's used, it's likely to be stolen."

"Sounds to me like you've got a professional on your hands, Inspector. You're going to need all the help you can get to find him," Jan said.

"I think you're right. Nice meeting you, ladies."

Sam left the shop and paused on the front step to take a calming breath. Her mind was racing, unsure about which direction to take first.

"Hey, is everything all right?" Bob asked.

"Yeah, I think so. I'm wondering where we should begin our investigation."

"Simples, right? Well, we've already spoken to Rachel's husband, so we can rule that out."

"Shit, that reminds me, we didn't drop Rachel's phone off at the lab."

He snorted. "Er... we didn't get the chance to because things kind of snowballed after he left the station."

"I know. Bugger, we're still not sure if Halima has been abducted or not. I suppose we should head over to her address, see if there's anyone there. Failing that, we can check with the neighbours. They might be able to tell us who to contact."

"Might be worth asking Claire to search the socials, see what she can find, just to save a bit of time."

"Good call. You do that. I'll ask Liam and Oliver to oversee things here with SOCO. They can get the relevant statements from Ernie, Coleen and Jan while they're here."

"They're going to love that," Bob mumbled.

"Someone's got to do it. They might as well make themselves useful while they're still here." Sam relayed her instructions to Liam and Oliver and then got back in the car. "What did Claire have to say?"

"She checked Halima's Facebook page, and it's showing she has a fiancé called Rory Marx. She followed the lead back to his page, and his job was listed as an estate agent."

"That's brilliant. Do we know which one?"

"Claire's going to whiz through his timeline, see what she can find out and get back to us."

"What would we do without Claire?"

"Yeah, I often think the same. She's amazing. We've got Halima's address, so do you want to go over there first?"

"That's what I was thinking. While we're on the road, can you see what you can find out about Penny via her socials?"

"On it now." He removed his phone from his pocket. "She's got a boyfriend called Eddy Huddlestone. Ah, okay, according to this, he's a coffee shop manager in Workington. 'Bean Juice'—Jesus, some of the business names these days are a bit naff. Is it any wonder there are dozens of them going to the wall?"

Sam laughed. "You can be such a grumpy old bugger. Bean Juice is quite a good name. Maybe they serve health juices as well as coffee. Giving their customers the best of both worlds."

"Maybe, that would definitely make more sense to have a play on words like that."

"There, you see, I knew you'd come round to the possibility of accepting the name, sooner or later."

7

Halima's home was a semi-detached Victorian house, situated on a quiet street on the outskirts of Workington.

"Stay here," Sam said. "I'll check if anyone is in first."

"Fine by me, I'll keep searching the internet."

Sam knocked on the front door but, as expected, there was no answer. So, she nipped next door to ask the neighbours. The first door she tried also remained closed. She had more luck when she tried the house on the right of Halima's. Sam held her warrant card up for the woman in her forties to read. "Sorry to trouble you, I'm DI Sam Cobbs. I was wondering if you know where Rory works."

The woman frowned. "Rory, from next door?"

"Yes, sorry, I didn't make myself clear. Do you know the homeowners at all?"

"Yes, Halima works with my husband at the building society. He's the manager there."

"Ah, yes, I think I met him the other day when I called to speak to Halima."

"He told me he had to cover the counter while Halima chatted with the police."

"I don't suppose you happen to know where Rory works, do you?"

"Yes, at Turner's Estate Agents in Workington."

"That's great, thanks so much. Do you think he'll be there today?"

"More than likely. What's going on? My husband rang half an hour ago, furious that Halima hadn't shown up for work. I noticed her car was still parked outside the house. I called round there to see if she was ill and needed any help, but I didn't get an answer. Initially, I thought maybe Rory had dropped her off at work because her car wouldn't start or something, but when Alan told me she was a no-show..."

"That's why we need to have a chat with Rory. Thanks for your help." Sam returned to the car without furnishing the woman with any further details, sick of repeating herself already.

"Turner's, that's where he works," were the first words out of Bob's mouth when she got back in the car.

"Thanks, so I've been told. That woman is the wife of Halima's manager at the building society."

"Wow, that's a coincidence I wasn't expecting to hear."

"Yeah, not sure what to make of it myself, not something I would entertain doing, living next door to my boss, not in my wildest dreams."

They both laughed.

Ten minutes later, Sam parked the car in one of the allocated spaces behind the estate agency. "Glad you told me this was here, it's always a nightmare trying to find a space in this part of town."

"You're welcome. Blimey, I'm going to need to have a lie down soon. That's twice I've been useful today."

His comment earned him a dig in the ribs before they exited the car. When they entered the office, Sam was surprised to see so many people working there. A woman with red hair crossed the room to greet them.

"Hello, I'm Milly. How may I help?"

"Hello, Milly. I'm DI Sam Cobbs, and this is my partner, DS Bob

Jones. We were hoping to have a quiet word with Rory Marx, if he's around?"

"Oh, the police! Yes, he's out back, having a meeting with the boss. I'll let him know that you're here." She weaved her way through the numerous desks and went through an archway at the rear of the room. It wasn't long before she returned with a man in his thirties, wearing a grey suit.

"Hello, Milly said you wanted to speak with me?"

"Is there somewhere private where we can have a chat?" Sam smiled, trying to put him at ease.

"Umm... I suppose we could chance it in the staffroom. Not sure how messy it is, though."

"That'll be fine."

He led the way back through the archway and into a small room at the rear of the property which was home to a table, some chairs and a sink unit. "It's basic but suits our needs. Take a seat, if you want. I'll stand." He rested against the sink and folded his arms. "What's this about?"

Sam and Bob sat at the table, facing him. "It's to do with Halima," Sam began, "When was the last time you had any contact with her?"

"This morning. She set off early on her run. We got up at the same time. I had breakfast and then left at around seven to go to the gym before I came here. Why? Is there something wrong?"

"Halima hasn't shown up for work today."

"What? That's news to me. Her boss hasn't informed me, he's our neighbour."

"Maybe he was too focused on setting up for the day. I'm not sure if you're aware of this. We visited Halima at the building society yesterday, and he wasn't too keen on sitting behind the counter while we had a word with her."

He laughed. "Sounds about right. The less contact he has with customers, the better. Actually, Halima mentioned that two police officers had been to see her. It was about Amy and Emily, wasn't it?"

"That's right. Sorry to have to inform you, there have been further developments in the case overnight."

"Oh God, I'm not liking where this conversation is going."

"Sorry, let me clarify the situation for you. This morning, we received a visit at the station from Rachel Wagner's husband. He was there to report his wife missing."

He frowned and shuffled his position. "Okay…" He fell silent as the pieces slotted into place. "And now you're here to tell me that Halima has gone missing as well?"

"Possibly. We tried to call Halima at the building society, and when we were told that she hadn't shown up for work, it got me thinking."

"Thinking what? Oh God, you're not telling me she's been abducted, are you? Like Emily?"

"There's a distinct possibility that might be the case."

His arms unfolded, he turned to look out of the window and shook his head. "How is this possible?" He faced them once more and repeatedly shook his head. "These kinds of things aren't supposed to happen to ordinary people. Maybe to the rich and famous, celebrities even, but not to people like us, who have very little to offer anyone. Why? What is this person hoping to accomplish by kidnapping our wives and girlfriends?"

"That's what we're trying to establish. Is there anything you can tell us that might help our investigation?"

"Such as? I'm an estate agent, for fuck's sake, not a copper, that's your job. Hey, you haven't come all the way out here to accuse me, have you? I love Halima, we're considering getting married. Why the hell would I kidnap her?"

Sam raised her hands to calm him. "That's not our intention. First of all, the reason we're visiting you is to make you aware of the situation and, secondly, it's only right that we should question you, see what you know, if anything, about your girlfriend's disappearance."

"I didn't know she was missing, not until you told me. Why would I know anything? You've got this all wrong if you've come here to lay the blame at my door. I love her, worship her. I wouldn't dream of hurting her."

"I'm sorry, there's been a mistake. I'm not suggesting you're behind Halima going missing. What we need to know is if anything has happened in the last couple of months that has puzzled you, perhaps. Has Halima told you she's felt unnerved about anything or anyone? As if someone has been watching her or something similar."

"No, no and no. This is all news to me. Yes, we've discussed the fact that Emily was abducted and that someone put Amy in hospital, but that's as far as our conversation went. Neither of us had any inclination that Halima might be in danger as well. Why didn't you warn her that might be a possibility?"

"We just didn't think this would be the outcome. Our investigation began a few days ago, and very little in the way of evidence has come our way since." Sam chewed her lip, hesitating for a moment before she hit him with the other news that had just surfaced. "There's more. Again, we have not yet had confirmation of what's happened to Halima, not yet, but I have to tell you that, as well as Rachel going missing, we have proof that Penny has also been abducted within the last hour."

"Holy crap, are you being serious?"

"Unfortunately, yes, deadly serious."

"I can't believe this. Why?" he shouted. "Why?" He came towards them and flopped into one of the spare chairs.

Sam covered his hand with hers. "We don't know. At this stage, the more their family members can tell us, the quicker we're going to find them all."

He withdrew his hand from hers and covered his eyes. His shoulders shook. "What can I tell you? Halima wouldn't hurt anyone. She has the most beautiful soul that I've ever encountered. Has this person, the one who took her, has he been in touch with you?"

"No, we've had no contact with him. He obviously had a plan in place, his aim to round the girls up quickly. The only perplexing part has been the fact that he ran Amy down instead of abducting her like the others."

"I wonder why. God, this is incredible. I'm at a loss what to say or think. I know you're here to ask me if I might have any information for you. I haven't. We've been exceptionally happy the past six months, no arguments, no major fall outs. Like I said, we've even had conversations about planning a wedding."

"What about past boyfriends?"

"She hasn't really got any. She was keen on a bloke when she first left school, but that fizzled out within a few months after he announced he was moving down to Cornwall. I don't think they've been in touch since."

"How long have you been together?"

He considered the question. "I think it's been around five or six years. That's the reason I popped the question. We haven't got around to choosing a ring yet. We were waiting until we go on holiday, which is in a couple of weeks."

He glanced over his shoulder. Sam sensed that the emotion was probably overwhelming him again. "I feel for you. All I can tell you is that we're going to use every available resource at our disposal to find them."

He turned back to face them. "Surely you must have something to go on?"

"The lab is examining the footage from the first incident, involving Amy and Emily, and we've got another disc to drop off on our way back to the station, one that highlights Penny's abduction."

"What about this person's vehicle? If he's taken Halima and Penny in broad daylight, wouldn't someone have seen him?"

"They did, but he was disguised. He was wearing a hoodie pulled down over his face, and from what we've learnt so far, he's got a penchant for stealing cars and setting them alight after he's discarded them."

"Jeez, destroying any potential evidence in the process, am I right?"

"Exactly, that's what we're up against."

"If that's the case, what hope is there of us ever seeing the girls again?"

"We've got to cling on to that hope, ensure we think positively at all times. My team and I aren't used to giving up, especially at the start of an investigation."

"Thank you, that's reassuring."

"Does Halima have any other friends we can talk to, other than those we've already mentioned?"

"No, I don't think so. We both lead busy lives. She barely has enough time to keep up with Emily and the gang, let alone meeting up with anyone else on the side."

"Okay, I'm going to leave you one of my cards." She slid it across the table to him. "If the kidnapper contacts you, will you ring me?"

"Yes, of course, but what if the kidnapper warns me not to involve the police? That's usually how these things work in the movies."

"I would advise you to trust me and my team, but the choice will ultimately be down to you. Are Halima's parents alive?"

"Sadly not. They both passed away when she was in her late teens. Both victims of different forms of cancer. Why?"

"I was going to suggest getting in touch with them for support more than anything."

"I'll be all right. If I feel myself getting low, maybe I'll reach out to Rachel's husband, Tom. I've met him a couple of times."

"Sounds like a good idea to me. Also, you can always call me, day or night. Just remember that."

"Thanks, I will."

They all rose from their seats, and Rory showed them to the front door, where he shook their hands.

"Hopefully, we'll get back to you soon with some encouraging news to share."

"I'll pray that happens. Good luck. I hope you find them soon before... I don't even want to think about what might happen to her, to them."

"Try to think positively."

They left the office, and Sam didn't speak until she returned to the car. Her mobile rang. She answered it immediately once she saw Claire's name show up on the screen. "Hi, Claire, we're on our way back to base after informing Rory that we believe Halima has been abducted. What do you have for us?"

"Umm… it's bad news, ma'am. Er… maybe I should tell you when you get back."

"Sounds ominous. Don't tell me one of the girls' bodies has been found."

"No, sorry, it's nothing to do with the investigation. I think I should leave it and tell you in person."

"If you think that's for the best, we should be with you within ten to fifteen minutes."

"See you then."

Sam ended the call and cast a glance in Bob's direction. "What do you think that's about?"

He shrugged. "Sorry, mind-reading isn't one of my hidden talents. Shouldn't we get on the road?"

She pulled a face at him and reversed the car. "You can be such a grumpy fucker sometimes."

"And a jack of all trades at others."

Sam put her foot down and made it back to the station in record time. They ran up the stairs to find both Claire and Suzanna in tears.

"What's happened? Come on, ladies, you're worrying the life out of me."

"It's Alex…" Claire said before her throat closed up.

"What about him?" Dread shrouded Sam's shoulders. "Come on, please, will someone tell me what is going on?"

Suzanna stared at her and shook her head. "He's gone. His heart gave out, and they couldn't revive him."

Sam and Bob both fell into nearby chairs and stared at each other.

"He's gone!" Sam whispered.

Bob put his head in his hands. "I can't believe it. He seemed fine yesterday when we were discussing his illness and him needing to go in for an operation. Why did he have to go on a waiting list? Why didn't they take him in, there and then, and put him under the knife?"

"Shit! I don't know, life isn't fair at times, is it? Oh God, I wonder if someone at the hospital has told his son, Nigel, yet. He was due to arrive today. Do you think I should call him?"

"It depends if Alex had him down as his next of kin or not," Claire said. She blew her nose on a tissue and added, "Maybe leave it for a couple of minutes until the news has sunk in."

"Yeah, you're right. I'd more than likely break down mid-conversation."

The room fell silent until their two boisterous junior colleagues, Oliver and Liam, entered the office. They realised straight away that something serious had happened.

"What's up?" Oliver asked tentatively.

"Take a seat, gents. We've got some upsetting news for you."

They looked at each other, worried expressions reflected on their faces, as they took their seats.

Sam cleared her throat and said, "Sorry to have to inform you that Alex has passed away."

"What?" Oliver said, his eyes bulging.

"Apparently, his heart stopped and the team at the hospital couldn't revive him," Sam said.

"Did they even try?" Liam mumbled.

"That was uncalled for, Liam," Sam chastised him. "I'm sure they did everything they could for him."

Liam murmured an apology, which Sam accepted.

She excused herself and went into her office to make one of the most difficult calls she'd ever had to make.

After sitting at her desk for a few minutes, rehearsing what she had to say to Nigel, she rang the man. When he answered, it sounded like he was in the car.

"Hi, Nigel. This is Sam Cobbs again. Where are you?"

"I'm on the M74, just approaching the border. I managed to get out of my course, because of the circumstances, I should be at the hospital within a couple of hours. I persuaded my sister to join me. Say hi, Wendy."

"Hi, thanks for letting us know about Dad."

"Umm... you're welcome. Nigel, is it possible for you to pull over onto the hard shoulder? Is it convenient where you are?"

"It is, but why?"

"Just do as the inspector asked, Nigel," Wendy ordered.

Sam waited patiently for Nigel to make the manoeuvre and get back to her.

"Right, that's us stopped now, Inspector. Is everything okay with Dad?"

Sam let out an enormous sigh. "I've not long got back to the station myself. Upon my return, I was told that your father has passed away."

"He what?" Nigel shouted. At the same time, his sister started sobbing.

"I'm so sorry. My team and I are in total shock here. I thought it was imperative that you know immediately. I was hoping to catch you before you set off. My thoughts are with you and your family at this unbearably sad time."

"I'm gobsmacked. We did not know Dad was even ill and to be told out of the blue like this that he's gone..."

"I know. I wish I wasn't making this call. I really do."

"Is there any point in us continuing our journey?"

"We must, Nigel. I want to see him," Wendy insisted.

"I guess that answers my question."

"Please, take your time. I'd allow the news to sink in a bit longer before you get on the road again."

"I'm fine. I think the quicker we get there..."

"That's up to you," Sam said. "You've got my number. I'm here if you need me."

"Thank you, Sam," the siblings said in unison.

"Take care." Sam ended the call. She replaced the phone in the docking station and felt totally numb, as though every muscle in her body had tensed up. She'd never had a colleague, or member of her team, die on duty before and she had to admit that she was struggling with how to process the fact.

A light knock sounded on the door she'd left ajar. Bob poked his head into the room. "How did it go?"

"Come in, take a seat. He's on his way, just about to cross the border. He's travelling with his sister, Wendy. God, that was one of the hardest calls I've made in my career. Where do we go from here, Bob? I wish someone would tell me because I feel traumatised, unable to think straight."

"It's going to take us a while to comprehend this has happened, Sam, but as harsh as this might sound, we've got an important investigation to deal with. We'd be foolish to allow sentiment to get in the way when we have those women's lives at risk."

She listened and nodded. He was right, the show must go on. "How are the rest of the team out there?"

"I've told them to take ten minutes out to deal with their emotions. I think you should do the same and then we need to get back to work. Those girls are relying on us to find them, to bring them home safely."

Tears pricked her eyes, and she smiled at him, then reached across the table for his hand. They intertwined their fingers. "He was a good man. I feel guilty for not giving him a chance around here."

Bob tugged on her hand. "That's nonsense and you know it. Alex was Alex. Even his seven kids weren't that close to him. I'd class him as one of life's loners. He'll be missed around here, that's for sure."

"I agree. I'll be fine once I've been able to process it a bit more. Let me tackle some of my emails. That'll give me the distraction I need for a few minutes."

He squeezed her hand slightly, then let it go. "Okay, if you promise me you won't dwell on it?"

"You have my word. We should go for a drink after work."

"I'm up for it. I'll run it past the rest of the team."

"Thanks. I'll be out soon."

8

He listened at the top of the stairs. The girls were trying to communicate with each other. Although the soundproofing was significant, there was a certain amount of noise that escaped from the cells, presumably from the gap under the doors. He took a seat on the top step and continued to eavesdrop on their conversation. It didn't take him long to work out it was troublemaker Emily who was asking a lot of the questions.

"Has he hurt any of you?" Emily asked.

"Only when he kidnapped me," Penny replied.

"Same here," Rachel said.

"Me, too," Halima said and then asked, "Does anyone know what this is about?"

A couple of the girls said no, but Emily didn't respond.

"Emily, do you know?" Rachel asked.

"Not really. It might have something to do with the story I've been chasing up."

"I thought as much," Halima said. "You hinted you were getting close to spilling the beans the night we went out, didn't you?"

"I'm sorry you ladies are involved. Hang in there, we can get out of this," Emily assured them all.

"How can you say that when this person won't even talk to us? How do you propose we get him to do that?" Penny asked.

He covered his mouth, deadening the snigger that was threatening to escape. It was thrilling to hear what was being said. He'd been right all along. Emily was getting closer to his tail. It was only a matter of time before she'd have closed in on him and run the story that would have impacted his life for good. Possibly turned his world upside down, maybe enough to have driven him out of town, if the police hadn't caught up with him first.

He hadn't realised the career Emily had chosen for herself in the years since they'd been out of touch. They'd known each other at secondary school, all of them. He'd been a recluse back then, happy to sit back and observe what the other kids got up to. Intentionally keeping under the radar, until one day Emily and her friends spotted him innocently watching them playing a game of netball after school. The teacher was late. He'd been spying on them from behind a shed. Emily had discovered him herself when the ball had bounced past him.

He'd crapped himself, frozen to the spot. She'd rounded the corner and stopped dead.

"You? What the fuck are you doing here?" She'd pounced on him without giving him the chance to either respond or to run off. Emily pinched his ear and refused to let go, putting enough force on it to make him move. "Hey, girls, look who I found behind the shed, gawping at us. We've got our own peeping Tom on our hands."

"Please, I wasn't. Yes, I was watching you, but not like that. You're all so good. I was admiring your ball skills, that was all. Let me go, please."

Emily squeezed tighter on the bony part of the ear, inches above his lobe, and laughed. "Did you hear that, girls? He was admiring our ball skills."

The group all laughed.

Emily got in his face and sneered, "Whilst trying to get a peek at our knickers, eh?"

"No, no, you've got this all wrong. I love the game, wish I could play, but netball is a girls' sport, not for boys. That's what Mr Munroe keeps telling us."

"So, instead, you thought you'd come down here after school to spy on us, to get a cheap thrill into the bargain, eh?"

"No, no, that's not right. Please, you have to believe me," he'd countered, his heart racing. Any form of confrontation paralysed him with fear. His shyness rendered him speechless most of the time. Even then, standing there, on the verge of pissing himself, grovelling to them was making the situation ten times worse for him.

"We don't have to believe anything from a creep like you. I've seen you before, skulking around, pretending you haven't been watching us when someone looked your way. How stupid do you think we are?"

"You're not. I'm the stupid one. Please, let me go."

"You've got that right. Why should we let you go? If you think we're mistreating you, you wait and see what Miss Luxton has to say about you sneaking around, spying on us. She'll make a right show of you in assembly tomorrow, you know what she's like. She detests boys like you. She'd swallow you whole if she could. I'm pretty sure of it." Emily had laughed, which had set the others off.

That's when he'd wet himself.

One of the other girls, Amy, had pointed out his accident to the others. He'd been mortified and squirmed to try to escape Emily's clutches, but her grip tightened on his ear.

The girls laughed and mocked him for the next ten minutes, and with tears streaming down his face, he'd pleaded with them over and over to let him go, all the while feeling uncomfortable in his soaking wet trousers. He'd never experienced such humiliation, ever.

He shook the vile image from his head and narrowed his eyes.

Now it's time to get my revenge. Now I have the courage to deal with them, to punish them.

"I'm scared," Penny said after the group had been silent for a few minutes.

"There's no need," Emily tried to reassure her. "We're here, together. There's strength in numbers, girls, we need to remember that. Don't let the bastard grind us down."

He chuckled and left the cellar, making sure that he slammed the door behind him, which he knew would spark another conversation between the group. He suspected it would be one filled with panic.

Good, they need to fear me. I have numerous atrocious plans ahead, ones that will ensure only the fittest will survive. First, I need to put the finishing touches to my notes. He rubbed his hands together, relishing the friction it caused.

But first, he would need to feed the women. He set about making ham sandwiches on white bread for all of them, aware that some of them wouldn't touch their lunch; most women these days, or the ones he knew, refused to touch carbohydrates. He chuckled. It was all part of the plan. The more they refused to eat, the weaker they became. *There's a method to my madness!*

He busied himself in the kitchen for the next fifteen minutes; at the same time, he went over his plan and made the odd note on the pad beside him. As his plan developed, so did the thrill of what lay ahead of him. *Revenge is sweet. I wonder where that saying came from. I must look it up one day. For now, I'll simply enjoy the moment.*

He filled four glasses with water and put those on the tray along with the sandwiches that he'd piled on top of each other, then he sucked in a deep breath, opened the cellar door and descended the stairs. He put the tray on the floor beside the first door and unlocked it. Before he stepped into the room, he collected from the corner the electric cattle prod he'd recently purchased online.

Halima rushed over to the bed and wrapped her arms around her legs. He deposited her sandwich and a glass of water on the side table next to her. "Eat it or don't. It's your choice. That's all the food you'll be getting today."

"I don't eat ham," Halima whispered.

"That's simple." He lifted the top slice of bread and removed the meat which he ate himself. Once he'd finished his mouthful, he grinned and said, "That solves that problem. Now eat it."

His erection grew when he noticed the fear resonating in her tearful eyes. He leaned in and whispered, "Don't worry, little one, all this will be over soon."

"Will it? Why are you holding us here?"

He winked at her, his mask still in place and, in a singsong voice, he said, "All will be revealed soon enough. There's no need for you to fret. I have something special lined up for you. Now, eat what's left of your sandwich."

Halima trembled and replied, "I will. Thank you."

He left the cell, secured the door behind him, then moved on to the next one. This time Rachel was the recipient of the lunch on offer. He opened the door and again entered the room with the threat of what the cattle prod was capable of, to prevent the woman from attacking him. "Lunch is served. If you don't eat it, that's your loss. It's going to be your one and only meal today. I'm a busy man and I have a few errands to run this afternoon. There are certain items I need to collect from the hardware store. Still, the less you know about that, the better. Eat up."

"When are you going to let us go? Our families will be worried about us."

He laughed. "I'm sure they are, but you know as well as I do how useless our police force is these days."

"No, don't leave. I'll do anything to secure my freedom."

He paused and turned to face her, his gaze running the length of her slim body. "I'll bear that in mind. Now eat your meal."

Keen to leave Emily until last, he opened the door to find Penny pinned against the wall right beside him, but the minute she saw the cattle prod, she rushed over to the bed.

"That was an extremely wise move you've just made. These things can be very effective when touched in the right place." He laughed and placed her sandwich and drink on the table beside her. "As I've told the others, this is the only meal you'll be getting today, so make sure you eat every scrap."

"Thank you. Why are you doing this to us? What have we ever done to you to make you hate us this much?"

"You'll know soon, I promise you. In the meantime, eat your meal."

He left the cell and prepared for the attack he knew was coming once he opened the final cell. Emily had always been a feisty bitch. From the moment he'd laid eyes on her, he'd realised that she was more than a match for him. However, his admiration for her had grown over the years, despite the humiliation she'd taken pleasure inflicting, not once, but several more times after the netball incident. Even though, at the time, the unkindness she'd shown towards him had hurt him, it hadn't prevented him from admiring how she always handled herself and what she'd accomplished in her life since she'd left school.

With the cattle prod at the ready, he left the sandwich and drink on the concrete floor and opened the door. Emily immediately pounced. She tried to knock the cattle prod out of his hand, but he was ready for her. He'd expected the move and held on tightly to the bar.

"Get back, I'm warning you. Unless you want to suffer later, you'll know what's good for you and get back."

Emily's gaze latched on to his. For a moment, he swore he saw a glimmer of recognition fill her eyes. The next second it was gone, and relief flooded through him once more.

Reluctantly, Emily released her grip on the cattle prod. "Why won't you reveal yourself to us? What have you got to hide? Do we know you?"

He laughed and gestured for her to get on the bed. "All will be revealed soon, my love."

Her mouth twisted, and she glared at him. "Don't call me that. If you have something to say, let's hear it. Otherwise, let us go, all of us."

"Oh, and who put you in charge, my love?" he repeated, amused by her enraged reaction.

"Have the courage to show yourself, if you're who I think you are."

So, the cat is out of the bag; you do recognise me. "And who might that be?" he challenged. He aimed the cattle prod at her stomach. She chose not to answer. "Come now, you seem to have all the answers, or think you do. Don't stop there, let's have it, if you dare."

"I refuse to give you the upper hand in this situation."

"You make me laugh. You always were an arrogant bitch."

"And you were..." She paused as the rod inched closer to her midriff.

"Go on, don't stop there. I'm having fun, aren't you?"

"What do you think, tosser?"

He prodded her in the stomach with the rod. Her scream was bloodcurdling for a split second before she slapped a hand over her mouth.

"I warned you. You should listen next time, it'll save you from getting injured... for now. Right, I must fly. I have people to see and places I need to be while you and your friends are otherwise engaged. Is there any point in giving you your sandwich and drink?"

"Fuck off. I don't want or need anything from you. I'd rather starve to death than eat anything you prepared. It'll probably be laced with poison anyway."

He gasped. "Wow, now that's something I hadn't thought about doing. Thanks for the tip. Maybe I'll play Russian roulette with the next round of meals I deliver, lace one of them with arsenic and see who has the courage to eat it."

"You're an evil bastard. Is this how you treated all the other women?"

He cocked an eyebrow and smirked behind the mask. "Now that would be telling, wouldn't it?"

"See, I know everything there is to know about you. The others might not recognise you, but I do."

"That's because your powers of perception are second to none. I've always admired that in you, my love."

"Screw you. The last thing I need or want is your fucking admiration." Emily shuddered under his intense gaze. "You make my skin crawl. You always have."

Her rudeness made him react. He prodded her again, once on each thigh. Emily clasped her hand over her mouth to suppress her screams, but he could see the defiance blazing in her eyes.

"You won't get the better of me, Emily. I recognise how resilient you can be. However, when the games begin, my love, you're going to need to drop your barriers and fight for your life."

He left the room and laughed his way to the top of the stairs, where he slammed the door behind him once more.

9

Sam and the team remained shell-shocked by the news they had received about Alex but, at the same time, they were determined to knuckle down and solve the case of the missing women.

Once Oliver and Liam returned to the station, Sam ordered them to take Rachel's phone, along with the footage they had copied from Ernie, to the lab. The results were hit and miss nowadays, what with staff shortages to contend with, so there was no telling when they'd hear from the lab. Sam hoped it wouldn't be too long because she felt the phone, in particular, could hold vital clues, but then again, she'd been wrong in the past. Rarely, thankfully.

"How are you holding up?" Bob whispered as he passed by the desk she had claimed in the outer office. It was the fourth time he'd asked her the same question within the last couple of hours and, although he meant well, he was ticking her off.

"I'm fine. There's no need for you to worry about me. Let's just concentrate on the case for now, Bob."

"Umm... I have a suggestion to make. Don't go snapping my head off, though."

She placed a hand over her heart. "Me? Would I do such a thing?"

He cocked an eyebrow. "Moving on. Have you told DCI Armstrong yet?"

Sam closed her eyes, realising her mistake, and swept a hand across her brow. "Shit. I knew there was something at the back of my mind that I had to do." She flew out of her chair towards the door. "Come and fetch me if I'm not back within ten minutes. Make up some kind of excuse, if you have to."

"Will do. Good luck."

"Thanks," she mumbled. By now, she was halfway to the chief's office. She ran through what she needed to tell him. No matter how many times she thought about it, the words sounded insignificant and hollow.

The chief's secretary, Heidi, glanced up, surprised to see her. "Hello, Inspector Cobbs. What brings you this way?"

"Sorry to interrupt like this, Heidi. I need to see him. Any chance? Or is he busy?"

"He's in a meeting with someone at the moment. I don't think he'll be much longer. Why don't you take a seat?"

Sam nodded and sat on one of the comfy padded chairs next to the coffee table. Needing something to keep her hands busy, she reached for a policing magazine and flicked through it. Moments later, the chief's door opened, and a man she often saw walking the corridors of the station emerged. They shook hands, and the man nodded at her before he left.

The chief approached her and, without smiling, he said, "Hello, Sam. I wasn't aware that we had a meeting scheduled for today."

"We haven't, sir. I dropped by on the off-chance that you'd have time to see me."

He inclined his head. "About?"

She lowered her voice to say, "A personal matter. It would be better if I told you in your office, sir."

"Very well, come through. Do you want a coffee? By the sounds of it, I think I'm going to need one. If you'd do the honours, Heidi?"

"Thank you, I'd love one," Sam responded.

"I'll bring them through," Heidi replied and rose from her chair to carry out the task.

Alan Armstrong huffed and puffed his way through his office to his seat. "I suppose this is to do with your fiancé, is it?"

"No, nothing could be further from the truth. He's doing well. Thanks for asking."

"Sorry, I've been snowed under lately. You have no idea what it's like for us when a new government is elected, especially one that hasn't been in power for over fifteen years. Everything gets turned on its head. The new Home Secretary is determined to make an impact. She wants to know the ins and outs of a duck's arse."

"I can imagine. I'm here to tell you..."

Before she could complete her sentence, Heidi entered the room with their drinks. She placed a bone china cup and saucer in front of Sam and another in front of the chief. They both thanked her, and Heidi left the room.

The chief gestured with his hand for Sam to tell him what was on her mind.

Sam swallowed down the lump that had been lingering in her throat since Claire had shared the news with her. "It's about a member of my team."

Armstrong interlocked his fingers and reclined in his chair. "Someone giving you problems, are they, Sam?"

Her chin dipped to her chest. The words she had rehearsed all vanished into thin air.

"Inspector? This isn't like you, to be lost for words. Has something serious happened?" His tone was softer, surprising her. "You're worrying me now. Come on, I can't help you if you don't tell me."

Tears misted her eyes, and she raised her head to look at him. "It's Alex Dougall, sir."

"What about him?"

"I'm sorry to have to inform you he passed away earlier today."

Armstrong sat upright and stared open-mouthed at her for a moment or two. After he regained his composure, he said, "What? How? Did an operation go wrong?"

"No, sir. Yesterday he revealed he had a heart problem. He'd hidden it from me and the rest of the team. He informed me that the hospital was going to give him a heart bypass. We were all dumbstruck but wished him all the best. He was due to speak with someone from HR about retiring. However, he didn't show up for work this morning. My sixth sense told me something was wrong. Several members of my team had tried to contact him, but he wasn't answering his phone. I sent Oliver around there to check he was all right. He wasn't. Oliver saw Alex flat out on the floor of his living room and called for an ambulance. Alex regained consciousness, and they transferred him to the hospital. We all went about our duties, knowing that he was in safe hands. Bob and I returned from interviewing a family member of a woman who was reported missing, to be told that Alex had passed away."

"Good grief. And you had no inkling that he was even ill?"

"No. He's always been the type to keep to himself around the office. Had I known he had heart problems, I would have insisted he got a medical right away. It's not something that should ever have been taken lightly by anyone, especially a man of his age. My grandfather had a heart attack at fifty-six, and he was forced to retire at that age."

"I don't know what to say. This has come as a total shock to me."

"It has to all of us, sir. The entire team is in there now, functioning on autopilot."

"Send them home early, if you have to."

"We're too professional to consider chucking in the towel, sir. We've already arranged to go to the pub after work. To give Alex a good send-off. Until then, we need to plough on as usual."

"You're to be admired, all of you. Pass on my thanks to the others." He stood and removed his wallet from the back pocket of his trousers. He handed her forty quid. "Have a drink on me."

Sam took the money, shocked that he would offer. "Are you sure?"

"Yes. I didn't know the man that well myself, but if he was a part of your team, then I'm sure he was a good worker."

Sam smiled. "He had his moments. Thank you, sir. I'm sure the others will appreciate your kind gesture, too. Would you like to come along?"

"Ordinarily, I wouldn't hesitate to be there, but I've got an official dinner I need to attend at the town hall this evening. Don't ask, it's due to be all pomp and ceremony, not my usual cup of tea. Nevertheless, it goes with the territory."

"I feel for you." She sipped at her drink, unsure what else to say to him.

"I mean it, Sam. I'm sorry for your loss. It's never ideal to lose a good man. Will you need to fill his shoes?"

She replaced her cup in its saucer and said, "Most definitely, sir, the sooner the better. Umm... about that, I was wondering if I could pinch Nick Travis from reception."

"May I ask why?"

"We have an understanding that's hard to match. He appears to be in tune with the way I think. Besides that, I had already run the idea past him yesterday, to prepare for when Alex chose or was told to retire, not thinking for one minute that he'd bloody die on us."

"Oh, you did, did you? And what was his reaction to the offer?"

"He seemed to be up for it. In all honesty, I believe his talents could be put to better use. They're wasted dealing with the public on the front desk."

"I'll consider it and get back to you later. Tell me about the investigation you're working on at present."

"It's a tough one. If I'm honest, it's one that is driving me to distraction."

"May I ask why?"

"It started off with one woman being kidnapped while her friend was run over and put in hospital. As far as I know, she's still there, unconscious in the ICU. It soon escalated into something else entirely. Now we're searching for four ladies."

"What? Why haven't I seen anything about this on TV yet?"

She sighed and swept a hand around her neck. "Because I haven't had time to catch my breath, sir. I've been interviewing friends and families non-stop since the first incident occurred."

"I'm sorry. I didn't mean to insinuate that you weren't doing your best. I would never dream of doing that, not to one of my best officers. I know we haven't always seen eye to eye over the years, Sam, but there's been no doubt in my mind that you put your heart and soul into the job every day."

"Thanks, sir. That means a lot to hear you say that. It's always a team effort. I'm nothing without my colleagues behind me."

"Agreed. You've never been one to accept praise without mentioning it being a team effort. Have you discovered a connection between the victims? Or is it too early to say, yet?"

"All five women were together the night the first woman was abducted and the other one hospitalised."

"I see. Do you have any idea who is behind the kidnappings or what their motive is?"

"Not yet. We have footage of him capturing one woman; he was well disguised, wearing a hoodie covering his features."

"That's a damn nuisance. Anything on the vehicle he was driving?"

"It would appear that he steals cars at will, abducts his targets, and then sets fire to the vehicles."

"Sounds to me like you have a professional on your hands."

"Which is why we're struggling to get any kind of hold on the investigation. We've delivered several pieces of evidence to the lab, no idea when the results are likely to be back."

"Keep on top of them. My advice would be to hold a press conference in the immediate future."

"I'm trying to get my head around that, sir, what with everything else that has been going on this week."

"Are you talking about your fiancé? By the way, congratulations on your engagement. How is Rhys now?"

"Thanks. He's getting there. He was due to go back to work this week but froze the second he was due to leave the house. I don't envy him. The thought of dealing with other people's personal issues when you're struggling yourself is not something I would relish."

"Not the best job in the world, admittedly. Is he receiving any help?"

"Yes, he's been working with a colleague of his, someone he totally trusts."

"I'm sure he'll get back in the swing of things soon. Now, back to the investigation. Would you like me to sit alongside you during the appeal?"

His unusual suggestion flabbergasted Sam. "If you have the time, sir."

"I'll make time, if only to support you. Get things organised and run it past Heidi before you confirm the time. Make it today, if possible. Sounds like those women need our help. Any delays in getting the word out there could be detrimental to their well-being."

"I'll do my best and get back to you, or should I say Heidi?" She finished her drink and left her seat. "Thanks for understanding, sir." She waved the money at him. "And for the contribution for this evening."

"My pleasure. See you later."

Sam left the office, thanked Heidi for the coffee and groaned when she peered at her watch. It was already four o'clock. It would be pushing it if Jackie could organise a conference this late in the day. She fished out her phone and gave the press officer a call on the way back to the office.

"It's Sam, Jackie. You're going to love me."

"Bugger, what do you need? As if I didn't know, and when do you need it?"

"The usual and ASAP, meaning today, if possible."

"Bloody hell, even I have my limits, Sam."

"I know, but there's no one better suited to their job than you, my dear friend. If anyone can pull it off, you can."

"Creep. Leave it with me. Can you give me a brief rundown of the case?"

"Four women kidnapped and another one in hospital. Will that do you?"

"Fuck. I'm on it. I'll get back to you when I can."

"You've never let me down yet."

"That's it, pile on the pressure."

Sam ended the call and entered the office. She circulated the room to see what information the team had gathered in her absence or during the afternoon. "What about Emily's previous cases, Claire?"

"Sorry, boss, I've checked all the names involved in the crimes she reported on and, as far as I can tell, all those responsible have been banged up. Of course, that doesn't mean a thing, if there was someone on the periphery that Emily didn't know about. I'll keep checking, if that's what you want me to do?"

"Yes, stick with it, if you would, at least until something else comes our way."

"How long are you going to give the lab?" Bob asked.

Sam perched her backside on the desk beside him. "Not too long. It's too soon to chase them yet. I'll consider doing it at around lunchtime tomorrow, if you can remind me."

He nodded. "How did it go with the chief?"

"It went. He was as shocked as we were." She dipped her hand into her pocket and pulled out the forty quid Armstrong had given her. "He's contributed to our little farewell gathering this evening."

"That was decent of him. He didn't volunteer to show up then?"

"No, he wanted to, but he's got a function he needs to attend."

"Convenient."

Sam smiled. "I genuinely think he would have come, if he could. Which reminds me, I need to call Rhys. Let him know I'm going to be late this evening."

"Thanks for the prompt. I need to do the same with Abigail."

The other team members had also forgotten, and they all got on the phone to their respective partners. Sam went through to her office to make her call in private. "Hi, love. How are you?"

"Improving daily. How's it going at your end?" Rhys asked.

Sam couldn't help but be buoyed by his tone. It sounded brighter than it had done in a while, or at least since the attack. "I hate to tell you this, but I'm going to be late this evening."

"Oh, any particular reason? Are you closing in on a suspect?"

"No, it's not work related, not in that sense. Er... we lost a member of our team today, Alex. Sadly, he passed away this morning, after Oliver found him unconscious at his home."

"Shit, that's crappy news. I'm so sorry, Sam. Will you pass on my condolences to the rest of your team?"

"I'll do that. We're going to stop off at the pub over the road before we head home, if that's okay with you?"

"Christ, you don't have to ask for my permission about things like that, love, just do it."

"It wouldn't feel right if I didn't. Thanks for understanding, Rhys. I won't be too long, I promise. What shall we have for dinner tonight?"

"Ah, well, I've cheated. I stopped off at that new pie shop in Workington and picked up a couple of steak and kidneys. I hope that's okay with you?"

"Yummy; oh heck, that reminds me. I don't think we had time to stop for lunch today. I need to apologise to the others, not that we've had time to shove a sandwich down our necks. Sorry, Rhys, I have to go. I'm waiting for a call from the press officer."

"Good luck. Take care driving home."

"Don't worry, I'll only have the one."

"I love you."

"Ditto. See you later." She ended the call just in time because her landline rang. "DI Sam Cobbs, how may I help?"

"It's Jackie. Can you be downstairs in half an hour, at four-forty-five?"

"Blimey, you don't hang around. Of course I'll be there. I forgot to tell you DCI Armstrong will be joining me for the conference."

"That's unusual. Can I ask why?"

"I should have told you earlier, we lost a member of our team today. He offered to give me some moral support, and I jumped at the chance."

"Oh, Sam, I'm mortified to hear that. Sending you a virtual hug."

"Thanks, gratefully received. I'll see you soon."

Sam hung up and sat back to ponder before realising that she needed to inform Heidi of the arrangements.

"Heidi, sorry to trouble you. DCI Armstrong asked me to inform you when I had confirmation of the press conference."

"That's right. He mentioned it to me after you left. Any luck, Inspector?"

"Yes, Jackie came up trumps and has arranged it for four-forty-five this evening."

Heidi tutted. "He's got a meeting at four-thirty. I'll see if he wants to rearrange that for another day."

"Okay, can you get back to me?"

"I'll do that."

Sam opened up her email tab on her computer to find it was clear for a change.

True to her word, Heidi rang her back within a few minutes, confirming that the chief would join Sam for the conference at four-forty-five. She spent the next half an hour jotting down copious notes, aware that her boss would expect her to be on top form, even though her mind might be elsewhere during the appeal.

Bob poked his head into the room at four-forty. "I know how keen you usually are to meet up with Jackie before you bare your soul to the press. Just letting you know you've got five minutes until countdown."

"Bugger, thanks for the warning. I hope the chief doesn't keep us waiting."

"I won't," Armstrong said from the other side of the door.

"Sorry," Bob mouthed when Sam cringed.

"Shit! Shit! Shit!" she mouthed in response. She did her best to brush the embarrassing episode aside, gathered her notebook and pen, then left the office. "Hello, sir. Please accept my apology..."

"Accepted. Hadn't we better crack on? We don't want to keep the pack of wolves waiting, do we, Inspector?" He turned on his heel, expecting Sam to follow him.

She virtually had to jog to keep up with his long strides all the way down the stairs. In the anteroom, she breathlessly introduced Jackie to Armstrong, unsure whether they'd ever met before.

He glanced at his watch and said, "I'm well aware who Miss Penrose is, thank you, Inspector. Is everyone here?"

"Just about, I think," Jackie responded.

The chief led the way onto the stage. A cloth with the station's number was draped over the two tables that Jackie's expert team had pushed together. Jackie kicked off the conference by introducing Sam and the chief, but it was Sam's responsibility to disclose the reason for the appeal.

The second Sam had stopped speaking, a few of the more outspoken journalists took it in turns to bombard them with questions.

"What's this person's motive?"

"Is there any indication of who this person is?"

"Does this have anything to do with Emily Burke's eagerness to follow up on stories that often involve criminal activity?"

Sam did her best to answer the queries until the chief stepped in to conclude the conference.

"If anyone has seen these four women in the last forty-eight hours," Sam pointed to the photos Jackie had erected on the wall behind them. "Please, please contact the station immediately and ask for DI Sam Cobbs or a member of my team. We are relying on you, the public, to help us."

The journalist who usually had it in for Sam stood and asked, "Why, Inspector? Can't you cope?"

"It's not that at all. You know how important it is to get the news out about criminal offences of this nature, Mr Edmonds. The more people who are aware of the situation, the more likely it is that we will find these women before... it's too late."

"And that completes this conference," the chief announced before the other journalists started aiming for the jugular, which was often the case once one of their associates had resorted to such tactics. "Thank you all for turning up at such short notice. We appreciate how seriously you're taking this, as are we. Any help you can give us will be a comfort to the families who are desperate to see their loved ones returned unharmed."

Armstrong left the stage with Sam while Jackie also thanked the journalists for attending. She joined them in the anteroom a few seconds afterwards.

"Not to sound condescending, but you're both to be congratulated for the way you handled the conference between you."

"Teamwork, eh, Inspector? I must fly. Thank you again for coming up trumps for us today, Miss Penrose."

"It's my pleasure, DCI Armstrong."

He marched out of the room, and Sam let out a relieved sigh and sank into the nearby chair. "Jesus, my heart was beating ten to the dozen up there, sitting next to him. I was praying I didn't get tongue-tied. God, how on earth did I get through that? It's been a day from hell without having to go through that ordeal."

Jackie smiled. "You're always the utter professional, Sam, despite what you think to the contrary."

"You're only saying that to make me feel better."

"Bullshit. I tell it as it is, always have done."

"That's sweet of you. Let's hope we get some joy from the appeal because we're getting nowhere fast with the investigation."

"Go home and get some rest. Like you said, you've had a hell of a day."

"I can't. The team and I have agreed to give Alex a send-off at the pub after work. You're welcome to join us, if you want."

"I'm going to have to pass, sorry. Duty calls at home. It's Mum and Dad's thirtieth anniversary, and we're having a family get-together at a local restaurant to celebrate."

"Aww, how wonderful. Wish them all the best from me, won't you?"

"I will. Come on, I'll walk back upstairs with you."

10

He returned from his shopping trip and laid out the tools he'd purchased, delighted that he was now ready to take his plan to the next level. He let out a sinister laugh as the thrill of the mission ahead took hold. He ran his hand over the tools, the coldness of the metal to his touch adding to his excitement. It would be a couple of hours before he could finally put his plan into action. For now, he fixed himself something to eat, hungrier than he thought he'd be after his excursion, until he realised he hadn't eaten anything at lunchtime, apart from the thin piece of ham he'd consumed after Halima had rejected it.

Removing the ingredients from the shopping bag, he switched on the radio and danced along with the tunes from the noughties that he enjoyed listening to above any other era, while he chopped and diced the ingredients and threw them in a frying pan. Within half an hour he was tucking in to a chicken Thai green curry and rice, savouring every morsel as it slid down his throat. Pleased with the results of his efforts, he washed his food down with a can of lager, then cleared up the kitchen.

Glancing at his watch, he decided he had time for a thirty-minute snooze, which he felt was needed after his exertions of trawling round the supermarket, dealing with dozens of shoppers, mostly inept morons who insisted on getting in his way. In a hurry, he had neither the time nor patience to deal with such people.

He felt refreshed after his nap and ready to take on the world. Wrapping the tools in a tea towel, he opened the cellar and listened. The women were silent. He descended the stairs and began setting up his equipment, before making several more trips upstairs to collect four kitchen chairs, which he used to form a circle.

"Hello, who's there? Please, let us go," Emily's voice was easily recognisable. She was the only one who had kept her fear in check every time she opened her mouth. The other girls took their cue from her and also pleaded to be set free.

"Hush now," he shouted, ensuring they all heard him through the gap under each of the doors. "I have something special planned for you. Have patience, and all will become clear in a few minutes."

The cellar fell silent once more. He chuckled, imagining the distress rippling through each of the women as the excitement grew within him. This wasn't the first time he'd abducted and tortured a woman, but it was the first time he'd collected a group of women, and the pleasure it was evoking was making his nerve endings quiver.

Within ten minutes, he had assembled all the equipment needed for this evening's entertainment to be considered a success, at least to him. He had no one else to impress, only himself. He placed a stool from the kitchen in the middle of the circle. Lying next to it were the tools, all laid out neatly on a sheet on the ground. He ran a hand over them again and tingled with sheer joy. Anticipation was the key, for now, although he was sure that regret would hit him during the evening, aware that anything ever rarely went smoothly in his life.

Smiling, he collected the cattle prod from the corner and opened the first door, intending to leave Emily until last. He would invite the women to join him. He chose Halima to be first. Deep down, he quite liked her, granted, not as much as he liked, or admired, Emily, but the richness of her dark skin made her a close second.

"You can come out."

Hesitantly, she shuffled towards him. He stood back, allowing her room to pass.

"What now?" she asked meekly.

"Take a seat. Don't try any funny business, either, otherwise I'll have to shock you with my prod, and you know how that went down with the feisty Emily, don't you?"

"Please, why are you holding us here? What have we ever done to you?"

He was delighted that the others hadn't appeared to recognise him. Thankful that wearing the mask had worked, he was further surprised that Emily hadn't divulged what she suspected. "Shut up and sit down. Do as I tell you or..."

Halima promptly sat on the padded chair and stared up at him, her eyes widening in fear. She seemed traumatised, and a little piece of his heart went out to her, but he gave himself a good talking-to, and the feeling soon vanished.

"What now?" her voice trembled, and her gaze shifted to the tools laid out on the cloth in the middle of the circle.

"Patience, my dear. Now you stay there; move and you know what will happen to you."

She nodded, her gaze following him across the cellar to the next door.

"Rachel, it's your turn." Again, he waved the cattle prod, intimating what was likely to happen if she tried to either run or attack him.

"What are you going to do with that thing?"

"That's down to you. Behave yourself and I won't hurt you. Try to escape and I'll be forced to use it and throw you back in your cell."

"I promise I won't try anything. None of us will. All we want is to go home to our loved ones."

He cocked an eyebrow. "Don't give me that bullshit." He tapped the side of his nose and winked at her. "I know, so don't try to pull the wool over my eyes."

Rachel frowned. "You know what?"

"I just know. This conversation is over. Sit there." He pointed at the chair to Halima's right.

Rachel stepped towards it and gave Halima a weak smile, which her friend returned. "Are you all right?"

"No talking. Don't push it, ladies. Sit there, in silence... or else."

Rachel and Halima stared at each other, beads of sweat breaking out on their foreheads and on their top lips.

Next up, it was Penny's turn. He opened the door to her cell and beckoned her with the cattle prod. "I'm warning you, like I've warned the others, any trouble and I'll poke you with this." He sneered and added, "I wouldn't advise it, if I were you. Take a seat next to Rachel. Put your hands where I can see them. That goes for all of you."

Penny scurried to her chair and glanced at Rachel, then Halima, but none of them said a word while he was within a few feet of them. He moved across the room to the last door. Prepared himself for the abuse he expected would come his way once he let Emily out of the room.

"What are you going to do with us?" Emily asked as she emerged from her cell and saw the other girls already seated.

"Stop asking ridiculous questions and sit down."

She remained defiant, glaring at him. He jerked the cattle prod in her direction several times, aiming at her stomach, and she leapt back, scared after her previous experience with the weapon.

"Sit down," he emphasised the words through gritted teeth.

Emily slipped into her chair.

"Hands where I can see them. Now."

She placed her trembling hands on her lap.

His nose wrinkled as the combined body odour of the women struck him. *Oops, I knew there would be something I'd forget.* He felt the need to apologise to his hostages. "Regarding the lack of washing facilities, I messed up. Sorry, ladies. Now, how nice is it to see each other?"

The women all stared at him, clearly afraid to speak in case he was toying with them, leading them into a trap.

"I am silly. I forgot to give you permission to speak." He smiled. "Answer me."

"It would be nicer still if you let us go so that we can be with our families," Emily said, her tone matching her defiant expression.

"Where would the fun be in that, Emily dearest? Aren't you wondering what I have in store for you all this evening?"

The women remained silent, even Emily.

"Ignoring me isn't the answer, ladies. You're spoiling my fun, oh, and making me seriously angry."

Emily gulped and asked, "What do you intend doing with us?"

He walked towards her, the cattle prod ready for action. "I'm not gonna do anything, you are."

Emily pointed at her chest. "Me?"

He smiled and nodded. "That's right. Now, get to your feet, slowly. One false move and you know what will happen."

Gingerly, Emily pushed herself out of the chair.

"We're going to play a little game. As you can see, you have several tools at your disposal. What you need to do is choose one to use on one of your friends. Each tool can only be used once. Do you understand the rules?"

Emily frowned and shook her head. "No."

"Tut-tut, Emily, and there was me thinking you were the brightest woman in this room."

"You're going to need to spell out what you want from me."

He jabbed the cattle prod at her, and she jumped back. "Treat me as a fool at your peril. Now choose a fucking tool, bearing in mind the rules. Halima will be your first victim."

"What? No, I don't want to go first," Halima screeched, tears streaming from her eyes.

He took a step to his right, all the time keeping his focus on Emily, just in case she did something reckless. "Shut up," he shouted in Halima's face. "I'm the one in charge. You'd be wise to remember that. The less you say, the more it will go in your favour. Have I made myself clear?"

Halima's chin trembled. "Yes, I'm sorry. It won't happen again.

Please forgive me. I'm scared. We all are. I miss my family. I want to go home."

His patience departed, and he prodded her on the thigh. Halima screamed. He turned swiftly, aware that Emily was out of sight behind him.

"Don't even think about it, Emily."

"I won't do anything against your wishes. Don't hurt us. Halima didn't deserve that. Please don't hurt her again."

"There's a solution to that. Carry out my instructions to the letter, and everything will be okay. If you don't, then I'll step in and punish your friends. Do you understand?"

Emily closed her eyes and nodded. "Yes. Okay, I'll do it."

"Emily, no! Don't listen to him. If we stick together, he can't hurt us," Rachel pleaded.

He was quick to react and aimed the bar at Rachel's neck. She yelled out as the pain erupted. He withdrew the prod, and she clutched a hand to her neck to cover the wound.

"Now, ladies, you're really starting to piss me off. Do you think this is some kind of joke? Believe me, in case you haven't realised it by now, I'm totally serious about this, which means you should be as well. Emily, this is your last chance. Choose your damn weapon."

There was no hesitation this time. Emily took a step forward and selected the pliers.

"Good choice," he said. "Now, I suggest you pull two fingernails from each of Halima's hands."

Emily glowered at him and shook her head. "I can't do it. Please, you can't make me. She's my friend. Friends don't do such violent things to each other."

"For Christ's sake," he groaned. "Just fucking do it or I'll do it to you. Take your pick."

"Oh God, no, I can't."

He aimed the prod at her thigh, got to within an inch of her flesh. "Do it."

Emily glared at him and, point-blank, refused.

The anger surged through him. He poked her with the cattle prod and then hit her with it several times. "You always were the one to cause problems back in the day."

"Leave her alone."

"Stop it, you're hurting her."

"Don't touch her. Emily!"

The girls shouted. It wasn't until Rachel got out of her seat and reached for the hammer that he regained his composure.

He turned to challenge Rachel with the cattle prod. "Don't even think about it, bitch."

Rachel stood her ground and challenged him. "Do your worst. Kill me. I'm not going down without a fight, none of us will. Grab a weapon, girls, he can't come after all of us. He hasn't got the balls for a start, have you, Price?"

He ripped off his mask. "That's right, it's me. The one you constantly mocked and made fun of at school. It's time for me to take my revenge."

"Except you can't even do a simple thing like that, can you? Look at you, you're nothing but a sad fucking individual, desperate to get his kicks any which way he can. Put the fucking prod down. I'm no longer scared of you. You've made a huge mistake, not restraining us out here, because we always stick together."

The other girls dived on the tools, each arming themselves with two items, ready to go into battle.

He spun around, constantly jabbing at each of them with his rod, but the girls took a step back, copying what Emily had managed to do with a huge amount of success. It wasn't long before his confused mind began playing tricks on him. His focus returned to Emily. He ran at her, letting loose a tirade of words. He chased her around the cellar.

The other girls urged Emily to run faster, but her legs soon gave out beneath her, her stamina waning quickly through lack of sustenance.

Price caught up with her and poked her twice with the cattle prod, momentarily forgetting they weren't alone until something whacked him on the back of the head and he tumbled to the floor.

. . .

"Oh, shit. What have I done?" Rachel kept repeating as she stared down at him, sprawled out at their feet.

"You've saved us," Penny said. "Come on, Rachel, we're wasting time. We need to get him in the cell before he wakes up."

The friends all dropped the tools they'd armed themselves with and pounced on either Price's arms or legs. Together, they heaved his body into the same cell Emily had been locked in. They closed the door behind them, and Emily had the satisfaction of turning the key to secure the bastard.

The friends hugged and cried. Glad their ordeal was over. Or was it?

"Come on, girls, we need to get out of here," Emily urged, and they ran towards the stairs, energised by the events that had unfolded.

11

Sam received the call at around eight that evening. She'd only been home for an hour and was winding down with a glass of wine and a cuddle on the sofa with Rhys. She groaned before she answered the call. "DI Sam Cobbs."

"Sorry, ma'am, this is Jason, the night desk sergeant. We've had an urgent call from a cab driver telling us he has Emily Burke and her friends beside his taxi. He's wondering what to do with them."

Sam sat upright and said, "You what? Can you repeat?"

"Emily Burke and her friends have been found."

"Holy crap. Are they hurt?"

"A few minor bruises, nothing major. What do you want me to do?"

"Can you send a couple of cars to collect them? I'll come back to the station now." She ended the call and punched the air. "My God, they've been found."

"That's unbelievable. What about the drink you've consumed? You can't drive. It would be too risky for you."

She smiled and fluttered her eyelashes at him. "Would you give me a lift? It shouldn't take long to sort things out at the other end. I can't leave things as they are until the morning."

He surprised her by bouncing out of his chair, she assumed eager to have a purpose. "I thought you'd never ask. Come on, what are you waiting for?"

"What about the dogs?" Sam asked.

"Shall I ask Doreen if she'll have them for a couple of hours?"

"Makes sense. I'd better get changed. I can't show up for work wearing this." She glanced down at the comfy leisure suit she was wearing. She shot up the stairs and heard the front door close. When she came down, the dogs were not there and Rhys was tying his shoelaces. "Was Doreen up for it?"

"Absolutely. She virtually snatched their leads out of my hand."

RHYS DROVE them to the station. As soon as they arrived, Jason brought Sam up to speed on where things stood with the girls.

"Two patrol cars picked the girls up. They're on their way back to the station now. They should be here any minute, ma'am."

"Thanks, Sergeant. It's such a relief to know they're safe. I wonder how they escaped and what's happened to the person who was holding them."

"The girls have said nothing to my men yet. They seem a bit dazed. I've sent another couple of cars out there to have a scout around. Once the girls tell us how they escaped, we'll have men out that way ready to swoop."

"They're probably in shock. Thanks for organising things so quickly, Sergeant."

Rhys took a seat, but Sam was too tense and wound up to join him. She ended up pacing the area for the next five minutes, driving Rhys and the desk sergeant mad into the bargain.

Eventually, Rhys tugged on her arm and urged her to sit.

"Sorry," she said, "I have a tendency to pace when I sense a situation is out of my hands."

"Chill. At least the women have been found and they appear to be mostly unhurt. You should be relieved about that, not anxious, love."

"I know you're right but..."

With that, the front door opened, and the area soon became flooded with women and uniformed officers. Sam tried to ignore the smell that accompanied the women, which suggested that they hadn't been treated well.

"Hello, ladies, it's good to have you back with us. I'm DI Sam Cobbs, the SIO on the investigation. First, does anyone need to see a doctor?"

"No, I think we're all right, although we could do with a shower and possibly a change of clothes, if that's okay?"

Sam smiled at the woman acting as the group's spokeswoman, who she faintly recognised. "Are you Emily?"

Emily's eyes watered. "Yes. Oh God, it's been terrible. We all tried hard to hold it together, but he... he was vile, kept threatening to torture us. He had a cattle prod he wasn't afraid to use to keep us in check."

"Ouch, I'm sorry you've been subjected to such an horrendous ordeal. Do you know the person who did this to you?"

"Yes, he went to school with us. He's called David Price. He was a creepy individual at school. It was only a matter of time before he broke cover and did something like this."

Sam inclined her head and asked, "What are you saying?"

"I've been following him for months, trying to gain the evidence I needed to run a story on the psycho."

"And that's what led us to getting involved," Rachel said, her tone accusatory.

Emily spun around to face her. "You believe this was all down to me?"

"You've just admitted it." Rachel turned her attention to Sam. "Look, I think we've all been through enough. As much as we want the bastard caught, I think I can speak for everyone: we're all desperate to go home, get out of these smelly clothes. Everything else can wait until tomorrow, can't it?"

"Of course, and that will happen as soon as you've given us a brief rundown of what unfolded tonight. How you escaped his clutches. I appreciate how desperate you must be to get home to your loved ones. If this man is still out there, it needs to be our priority to find him. I'm sure you'll agree, especially if he knows where all of you live and work."

"Shit, I never thought about that," Rachel replied. "Can't you put us up in a hotel or a safe house?"

"I can see what's available, but that's going to take time. I think you should have a shower at the station first, and we'll go from there. Perhaps I can have a chat with you once you've had your showers."

"The inspector is talking a lot of sense, Rach. The last thing you'd want is for him to show up at your house, especially if Tom isn't there," Emily said.

"Ah yes, he mentioned that he often works late," Sam jumped in.

Emily and Rachel both glanced her way.

"That's a lie. He's been cheating on Rachel for months," Emily declared.

"What? He came across as caring a lot about you when he was in here the other day. He came to the station to report you missing."

"Well, at least he's done one decent thing in the last six months, hey, Rach?"

"Shut up, Emily. What the fuck do you know about relationships? You've got a man who truly thinks the world of you, and you end up getting divorced. All these months later, I'm still trying to figure out how your marriage went tits up."

"It was because of her job," Halima stepped forward to add. "Your job has caused all this trouble as well, Emily. You're simply too wrapped up in your career to notice what's going on around you. Gerald told me it was like living with a woman who was possessed, and not in a good way. That man loves every inch of you. He'd have you back tomorrow if he could, and yet, half the time, you don't even know he's in the same room as you."

Emily held her head in shame. Lifting it again, she said, "Please don't make this all about me."

"Why shouldn't we? It's the truth," Penny said.

Sam moved to stand between them. "Please, you don't want to fall out about this. Leave the recriminations for another time. It's too raw at the moment. We can get a shower organised for you. In the meantime, I'll make arrangements for you to stay in a hotel this evening. How does that sound?"

The women all nodded.

"Can we ring our families? They'll be going out of their minds with worry," Halima said.

"I was about to suggest the same. Sergeant, are the interview rooms free?"

"They are, ma'am."

"I'll show you the way," Sam said and took them down the corridor, leaving Rhys behind. "Feel free to use the phones. Just dial nine for an external line."

The women all mumbled a thank you, and Sam left them to it. She collected Rhys from the reception area and went upstairs to her office.

"So, this is where all the excitement happens, is it?"

"Hey, it's not that impressive, and most of our day is spent at our desks, pulling our hair out."

"Okay, if you say so. I'm still super impressed, though, watching you in action. I witnessed how you took control of the situation downstairs, intervened before things escalated." He gathered her in his arms and kissed her.

She kissed him back and then released his grip around her waist. "As much as I'd love to spend the next ten minutes snogging your face off, I have an important task to complete."

He grinned. "Oh yes, of course you have. How about I make us some coffee, rather than stand around doing nothing?"

"Sounds just the ticket to me. Thanks for being here, Rhys. It means a lot to hear you say that."

"I'd leave the appreciation until you've tasted my coffee."

She laughed and walked into her office. "Come through when you've finished."

Sam spent the next ten minutes calling all the hotels in the area to enquire if any of them had enough rooms to put the girls up together, thinking it would be advantageous to have them all at the same premises overnight. After her fifth call, her frustration seeped away when the receptionist at The Lawns Hotel told her she had two family rooms available for the night, but they would be both occupied the following day. Rhys was sitting opposite her in awe. She could see his admiration sparkling in his eyes.

"Before you heap lots of praise on me, I'm only doing my job."

He held his mug close to his lips and said, "With professionalism and ease. You're amazing, Sam, and I simply don't tell you enough."

"Stop that! It's my job to take care of the public."

"Nope, you're going above and beyond. You just can't see it. Is there anything I can do?"

"No, you being here with me has been a bonus tonight. Thanks for agreeing to tag along."

"I'd volunteer to be your chauffeur every day of the week if it meant I could observe you in action from this side of the desk."

"Get out of here. We need to concentrate on getting you fit and back to work."

"I promise, I'm nearly there. The past couple of days, spending time with the dogs, walking in beautiful surroundings, has done me the world of good. We really don't know how lucky we are living here. It's not until you take your foot off the accelerator and get out there to explore that you realise what a fabulous area this is to live in."

"I'll have to take your word for that."

Rhys cringed. "Sorry, I didn't mean to rub it in. What's next on the agenda? Now that you've sorted out the accommodation for the women."

"I'll go downstairs, check how they all are, organise the shower rota for them and arrange for them to have a change of clothes. First, I need to have a quiet word with Emily, without the others pouncing on her."

"I'm guessing to see if she can give you any information about where they were held and who the suspect is?"

"She mentioned who he was and that they went to school together, but I'm going to need more than that if we're going to arrest him. I'm glad they didn't come to blows down there."

"I suppose that was bound to happen. They'll be looking for someone to blame, and Emily appears to be their prime target."

"I get that, but what's the point? There isn't one, not if they've come away from it relatively unscathed."

He tapped his head. "Their brains will be working overtime, trying to work out if there was anything they could have done differently."

"I know. Maybe we can help them out there, eh? Once you're back at work, no pressure, though."

"Not much. If nothing else, I can make them a decent cup of coffee. This stuff is vile. How do you put up with it every day?"

"Vile? You should have tasted the stuff that we were forced to endure before. It was rank. Made me heave every time I had a cup. This new blend is ten times better than its predecessor."

"Christ, poor you."

They finished their drinks and went back downstairs. Rhys was instructed to sit in the reception area with the promise that Sam wouldn't be long. She walked down the narrow corridor and paused at the sound of raised voices. She ran the rest of the way and barged into Interview Room One, only to find Emily had Rachel pinned up against the wall, Emily's forearm pressed against Rachel's throat. Sam rushed forward and pushed Emily off her friend.

"Cut it out. This is no way to behave, ladies."

Rachel coughed and held her hand to her throat. "You're fucking insane, Emily."

"Me? You're the one who is intent on blaming me for this damn fiasco. I had nothing to do with this. Price had a fixation on all of us. He was a nutter back in the day, a weirdo, you all know that."

Sam grabbed Emily's arm. "You and I need to have a chat in the other room."

Emily wrenched her arm out of Sam's grip. "We're wasting time here. Correction, you're wasting time. You should be out there, arresting the bastard."

"And we will, once we find out where he is."

"He's at the house. We locked him in the cellar."

"What? Why are you just telling me this now?" Sam led her into one of the other interview rooms and forced her to sit down.

There, Emily covered her face with her hands. "I don't know. I suppose we were all in shock because none of us expected to get out of there alive."

"All right. Back up. Where was he holding you?"

"In a house. We didn't know where it was until we escaped. It's got a cellar. He had some purpose-built rooms down there where he kept us locked up. I think they were soundproofed, although we managed to communicate with each other most of the time. He expected me to torture my friends. I couldn't do it. We fought back, and Rachel knocked him out with a hammer. We shoved him in one of the rooms, a cell he called it, and locked him in. Then we bolted out of the house and shouted for help. No one came to assist us. We wandered for a while and eventually flagged down a taxi. He helped us, he was the one who rang the police. No one else was willing to help us, though. What a shitty world we live in when people can ignore a woman's cries for help."

"I think you're right. Don't worry about that for now. You're safe, that's all that matters. Did you catch the address of the house? The number on the door as you were leaving?"

Emily closed her eyes and contemplated Sam's question. "I think it was number nineteen. It was in a cul-de-sac. I can't recall the name of the road. It wasn't too far from where we were found. Surely your men will find it."

"We're going to do our best. And the man holding you, you know him?"

"Yes, David Price. I got the impression that it wasn't his house… hang on, no, it's not. I found out recently that his parents lived there. Damn, why can't I remember the name of the road?"

"Try to relax. We'll find it, don't worry."

Emily clicked her fingers together. "Horseshoe Crescent, that's it."

Sam patted her hand. "Well done. I'll get some men over there ASAP."

Emily let out a relieved sigh, and her head flopped on to the table.

"Why? Why us? He says we mistreated him at school. I can't recall it happening that way. We caught him out a few times, spying on us, like when we were playing netball. He gave us the creeps. I never dreamt it would turn out like this, years later." She sobbed.

Sam allowed her to rid herself of the emotions overwhelming her, without interruption. Emily sat up and dried her eyes after a few minutes.

"All right now?" Sam asked.

"I'm sorry. I needed to get it out."

"I know. You've been through a hell of an ordeal. It's understandable that you should feel overcome. You're also dealing with the relief of escaping his clutches. You're to be admired, all of you, for the bravery you've shown getting away from him."

"It was either that or fight for our lives. He said he had some games planned for us. In the first one, I had to pick one of the tools he had laid on the floor and use it to torture my friends. I couldn't do it. I refused, and he poked me with the cattle prod. If it hadn't been for Rachel encouraging the other two to grab a weapon, we wouldn't be here today. They're the brave ones, not me."

"You're all brave. I know it's getting late and all you want to do is get your head down, but can you tell me what you had on Price?"

"I've been secretly following him for months. I suspected he was abducting women, but I needed the proof to give to my boss. He gave me the go-ahead to go after him, under strict instructions that I kept it from my colleagues."

"That was foolish of him—sorry, I have to add, and you. Any suspicious events, you should automatically call the police, if only to prevent situations like this from happening. I know you've got big boots to fill and that your father, in his day, was a top-class investigative journalist. What do you think he would say about you getting abducted? Putting not only your life, but also those of your friends, in jeopardy?"

"Don't go there. I'm dreading telling him. I've kept away from my parents over the last few months in case he pumped me for information about the latest story I was working on. He would have immediately worked out that I was keeping something from him."

"You didn't answer my question. What would he say about putting yourself, and your friends, in jeopardy?"

"He'd crucify me, which is why I've kept my distance from him and Mum. Look, I know I've screwed up. I'm going to have to live with the consequences of my dubious actions for the rest of my life. Furthermore, I've probably damaged the relationships I've had with my friends for the last twenty years or more. I'm gutted about that more than anything."

"Hopefully, once the dust has settled and we have Price in custody, it won't come to that. Who did you inform you were safe?"

She closed her eyes and swallowed, then opened them and said, "I don't know if I've done the right thing or not. My ex-husband. I listened to the girls. The night we went out for a drink, they made me realise that I've been so engrossed in my career over the years that I've failed to appreciate those around me, those who cared for me."

"Who loved you unreservedly? When I spoke with Gerald, it was written all over his face how much he loves you. I'm glad you called him."

Emily tipped her head back and puffed out her cheeks. "I've been an idiot, and it's time to make amends, not only to Gerald, but to my friends as well."

"Don't be too hard on yourself. If, or should I say when, we catch up with Price, can we count on you supplying us with the extra evidence we might need to convict him?"

"Absolutely. I no longer give a shit about the story I was hoping to write. If it'll help convict him, I'll willingly supply you the ammunition, should you need it."

"The other girls you mentioned, do you know what happened to them?"

"No. He's a devious bugger. I believe he knew I was tailing him when he left work at night. Sometimes he'd drive around for an hour or more, just to tick me off, I think."

"Where does he work?"

"At a dental practice in Whitehaven. We're all patients there."

"So that's how he gained access to your personal details, your addresses and where you work."

"Yes, I'm assuming so." Emily shuddered. "I can't get the image out of my mind of what he expected me to do to my friends. I'm glad we foiled his plan."

"Me, too. Let's get you sorted and settled at the hotel."

Sam returned Emily to her friends, who unfortunately lacked empathy and didn't exactly welcome her with open arms. Emily assured her she would make amends with the others; therefore, Sam went back to the reception area to have a word with Jason. "Can you arrange for a taxi to pick up the four girls and take them to The Lawns Hotel?"

"You don't want my guys to drop them off?"

"I think it would be better if they didn't show up in a police car."

"Ah, gotcha. Leave it with me, ma'am."

She approached Rhys, who was smiling at her.

"Are you having fun?" she asked. "You seem to be."

"It might be possible that I've missed my vocation in life. I think deep down I always wanted to be a copper. Being here tonight, watching you in action, has got my juices flowing again."

"Steady on, you have a successful career of your own waiting for you. I've decided to stick around for a while, at least until we arrest the suspect and bang him up in a cell. It wouldn't feel right just going home and dealing with it in the morning. So, if you want to shoot off, I'll jump in a cab later."

"Do I have to? Can't I stick around here and give you a hand?"

She was unsure whether she wanted that, and the conversation went back and forth for the next few minutes. It comprised of Sam mostly putting obstacles in his way as to why that wouldn't be such a good idea, but Rhys came back with an answer to combat her excuse, every damn time.

In the end, she shrugged and said, "It could be a late one. I mean, we might not leave here until the early hours of the morning."

"As long as I'm with you, I don't care. Call it an exercise in rehabilitation," he suggested.

"You're crazy, all right. Let me have a quick word with the sergeant. He'll need to note it down in the visitors' book, just in case we have a fire."

He nodded and beamed like a Cheshire cat.

After signing him in, Sam gestured for Rhys to join her upstairs. "There are a few phone calls we need to make between us. You'd better ring Doreen. Check if she's up to looking after the dogs for an extended period."

"I'll get on it now." He removed his mobile from his pocket and rang their neighbour.

Sam entered her office and rang her partner. "Hi, Bob, I'm only calling you to make you aware of the situation. I don't want you to come into work, do you hear me?"

"Oh hell, what's happened? And why are you back at the station?"

"Briefly, all the kidnapped women have been found."

"Thank God for that, but that really hasn't answered my question. If they've been found and are safe… they are safe, aren't they? Why is there any necessity for you to be back at work?"

"Yes, they're safe. Because I want to be here when they bring the suspect in. Uniformed officers are out there now, searching for the address."

"Christ, it sounds like a plot from one of those naff B-movies which are flooding TV at the moment."

Sam laughed. "Doesn't it? I'd better get on. Like I said, I just thought you should know."

"Give me your word that as soon as the suspect is caught, you'll shove him in a cell and head home for the night. We can interview the bastard together in the morning."

"You have my word. The adrenaline has kicked in and driving me right now. I have a feeling it will diminish soon."

"I've got no intention of going to bed yet. Will you call me later, let me know how you're getting on? You know I'll only worry about you if you don't."

"I can't promise that. You know how things can turn out when you least expect them to, but I'll try. Rhys is here with me, keeping me company."

"Whoa, is that even allowed?"

"Nope, but..." She giggled. "It is what it is. After our trip to the pub earlier and needing to get back to the station ASAP, I had no other option but to accept a lift from him."

"Hmm... there is such a thing as calling a taxi."

"All right, Mr Smartarse. I'm going now."

"Okay, good luck. Call me later, as promised."

"I said I would try. Don't fret about me. That's an order."

"Hard not to, boss."

She ended the call and was eager to know how Rhys had got on with Doreen. "Well, what did she say?"

"Bloody hell, I thought she was going to burst with joy. She told me she'd nip back to the house and collect their beds plus a few more treats for them as she's run out."

"I forgot I gave her a key. Not sure I like the sound of the treat part. Bless her, what would we do without her? She's such a sweetheart, and she adores our dogs."

"I agree. You definitely struck gold moving to that cottage."

"It's had its difficulties over the years. Mixed memories." A sadness crept up on her and draped around her shoulders. Rhys took a few steps towards her, but she placed a hand on his chest to ensure he gave her space. "I'm fine. Don't worry about me. I have a job to do."

"Okay, you have my permission to use me and abuse me while I'm here. I have no intention of sitting on my hands, doing sod all."

"If you insist, you might live to regret saying that, though. I'll start up a computer for you, if you promise not to snoop around on it."

A hand covered his chest, and his eyes sparkled. She was delighted to see the old Rhys emerging from the depths of despair he'd sunk to since the attack. However, she was also cautious about putting a dent in his newfound confidence and causing his recuperation to go backwards. "Not so fast, matey. I have a job to do. I'm going to be strictly professional from now on, got that?"

He saluted and flashed a cheeky grin. "Yes, boss." He exaggerated a shudder and whispered, "Even though you turn me on when you chastise me."

Sam doubled over in laughter. Straightening, she wiped away the tears and said, "As I was saying before your dirty mind sidetracked our conversation, I'll start up the computer. I'd like you to bring up the area where the girls were found. I need to see what's around Horseshoe Crescent, just in case he makes a run for it when he's picked up."

"Obvious question from me: how did the girls escape his clutches?"

"They took their chance to overpower him. While he was attacking Emily with a cattle prod, one of the other girls, Rachel, I think it was, clobbered Price with a hammer. That knocked him out, and together they threw him into one of the cells he'd made in the cellar."

"So, there's no chance he might wake up and find a way out of there if he built the rooms?"

"There are unknown variables at play here. I wouldn't like to say either way and end up with egg on my face. The sooner you get on with the research, the better. So, what are you waiting for? I'm not used to asking my colleagues twice to do something around here, once is usually enough."

He tried to keep a straight face. They both did.

"Consider me told." He plonked himself in the chair and brought up Google Maps. "Here it is. There are twelve, no, fourteen houses, in the crescent."

"She told me it was number nineteen. I just want to get a feel for it… scratch that, what am I thinking? Come on, let's get over there and join the patrol cars searching the area."

"I didn't realise you had the full address."

"Don't even go there. The drink has obviously had a greater impact on my judgement skills than I realised."

They ran back to reception.

Sam paused to speak to the desk sergeant. "Are your patrols at the location?"

"They're having a snoop around out there, ma'am."

"Okay, stay here," she ordered. Rhys opened his mouth to object until she clarified her intentions. "I'll be right back. I'm going to the armoury to pick up a Taser."

She sprinted up the corridor and returned moments later with a Taser in hand.

"Wow, can I have a look?" Rhys asked, his eyes as wide as a five-year-old's at Christmas.

She rolled her eyes. "Any trouble from you and I'll have no hesitation in using it," she jested.

The sergeant suppressed a laugh behind his hand.

"I wouldn't dream of it. I'm eager to see the damage you can do with that thing."

Another roll of the eyes, and she turned him around and pushed him gently through the main door.

"Sorry, did I embarrass you back there?"

"Not really. Although you probably gave Jason the best laugh he's had all month."

"Glad I brightened someone's day for them."

They arrived at the location to find two squad cars outside the property. Sam gave Rhys explicit instructions to remain in the car, out of harm's way, whatever happened. He adopted a serious demeanour and assured her he would abide by the rules she put in place when they were out in the field.

She removed her warrant card from her pocket and flashed it at the uniformed officers, who were all young males. "Thanks for attending. Are any of you Taser trained?"

Two of the officers raised their hands.

"Good. I collected one before I left the station. We're here to seize a dangerous criminal, so I'm going to need you to stay alert at all times and use your Taser if necessary. Did you find anything around the rear?"

"Nothing, we tried the back door. It was locked. The front door is ajar, but we haven't entered the property yet, because we were told to hold off and that you were on your way, ma'am."

"Let's change that and get in there. I'll take the lead. Don't be afraid to use your Tasers if the need arises. The last thing I want is this man escaping. He's a danger to our society."

Sam approached the house and, with her Taser drawn, eased the front door open and entered the hallway. She chose to advance silently rather than storm the property. It wasn't long before she located the cellar door, which was close to the kitchen. It was wide open. She tentatively descended the steps and inwardly groaned when she saw the time and effort that Price had put in to prepare this room. The cells that had been erected with the sole purpose of accommodating the hostages. The tools the girls had mentioned were strewn across the floor. A trail of the larger tools led to the staircase, suggesting that the women must have ditched them in their haste to leave the cellar.

Once Sam and the four officers had gathered in the cellar, she noticed that all the cell doors were open. She hadn't expected that. "I was told that the hostages overpowered the suspect, knocked him out and locked him in one of the cells."

"He probably had either a spare key or a master key on him, ma'am," one officer suggested.

Sam thumped her thigh and sighed. "You're probably right. I still think we should conduct a thorough search of the property, in case he's still here, before we put out an alert for him."

With the cellar drawing a blank, they returned to the ground floor. Sam left the officers to begin the search, ensuring they were paired up, with one Taser-trained officer in each couple. Then she headed back to the car to fill Rhys in.

"Shit, shit, shit! How could he have escaped?" Rhys asked.

"He must have had a spare key on him. Looks like it's going to be a long night. Maybe you should head home, hon."

"No, I'll stay with you. We can discuss the matter again in a couple of hours, if we haven't found him by then."

"I love the fact that you used *we* in that sentence as if we're a team."

"I thought we were." He grinned and leaned over for a sneaky kiss.

"You'll get me fired if you carry on doing that."

"Why? We're in my car."

"Okay, you win that round." She rubbed her tired eyes and shook her head. "Bugger, I really thought we had this investigation in the bag. I should have known there would be a damn twist in the tale. These things rarely go according to plan. I'm tired now. I doubt if I'll be able to cope for much longer out here anyway. Let me get back inside, see how the officers are doing in there, then we'll go back to the station and put our heads together."

"That sounds like an excellent idea to me."

Sam returned to the house to be told that the suspect hadn't been found. "Have you checked the attic?"

"Yes, ma'am. Nothing up there at all, which surprised us."

"Christ, I've never known a house with an empty loft before. Okay, we'll leave the door on the latch. SOCO will need to examine the place in the morning. Are you on duty for the rest of the night?"

"Yes, ma'am, until six."

"Right, will you continue to patrol the area overnight, just in case he comes back?"

"Is this his address?" the officer asked.

"No, it's his parents'." She nodded, understanding where the officer was leading. "We should drop over there. Can two of you come with me?"

The men decided between them who should accompany her. Sam looked up the address that Emily had given her earlier and gave it to the officers. Then she ran back to the car and inserted the postcode into Rhys' satnav. The route was calculated within seconds.

Sam tutted. "It's ten minutes from here. Bugger, I should have covered his address earlier."

"Sam, there's no point in blaming yourself. As far as you knew, he was here, unconscious."

"Yeah, you're right." She placed a hand over his on the steering wheel. "I'm glad you opted to stay with me. I'd hate to be out here doing this on my own."

He shot her a glance before returning his gaze to the road ahead. "What are you saying? That sometimes you go on dangerous missions alone?"

She cringed and slapped a hand to her cheek. "It has been known in the past, admittedly, but you'll be pleased to know it rarely happens."

"That's a bloody relief. I hate the thought of you being out here on your own, with the number of psychos out there walking the streets." He leaned over and added quietly, "And yes, that's experience talking. I can assure you I've had the privilege, that might be the wrong word, of plenty of people fitting into that category, on my couch, over the years."

"God, don't. Maybe we should revisit this conversation later. I could do with hitting my target this year to keep Armstrong off my back."

He gaped at her.

"What? I was joking. If you don't mind, I'd rather you keep your eyes on the road."

"Yes, boss. Anything you say, boss."

"All right, there's no need for you to go over the top. *Ssh*... I need to use the time during the journey to formulate a plan for when we get back to the station."

"Yes, boss." He grinned and winked at her.

She smiled and withdrew her notebook from her pocket.

He nudged her a couple of minutes later and said, "We're two minutes away from the house."

"Bloody hell, that was quick. You didn't break the speed limit to get here, did you?"

"I might have done, once or twice. Isn't that allowed when you have a copper sitting in your passenger seat?"

"Give me strength, and I thought Bob was a pain in the arse out in the field."

They both laughed.

"Charming, you can go off some people, you know."

"God, you are him. That's usually the type of crap he spouts, too, just saying."

Rhys shot her a toothy grin.

Not long after, Rhys pulled up outside Price's small, detached house on the outskirts of Workington. Sam made sure he understood how important it was for him to remain in the vehicle.

"I'm a seasoned pro by now. I know the drill. I'll sit here twiddling my fingers while all hell breaks loose inside."

"Crikey, I hope not. Hopefully, the Taser will be enough of a deterrent to prevent that kind of thing from happening. I love you."

"Shit, now I'm worried."

"Why?"

"Because you didn't say that before you got out of the car at his parents' house."

"Sorry, I thought about saying it. Does that count?"

"I suppose so. Any chance of a sneaky kiss for luck?"

"Do you think I'm going to need it?"

"I hope not. It wouldn't hurt, would it?"

Sam glanced over her shoulder at the car behind, pecked him on the lips, then threw the passenger door open and exited the vehicle. Studying the house, the thing that struck her most was that the inside of the property was in darkness. Granted, it was already approaching midnight, but all the same, something wasn't sitting right with her.

She met up with the two uniformed officers, and together they walked up the path to the front door. There was another path leading around the side of the house.

"Why don't you go around the back?" she said to the tallest officer.

He nodded and darted off.

"Are you ready for this?" Sam asked the other officer.

She was the only one carrying a Taser, which she held at her side, slightly behind her leg. She rang the bell but, as expected, the door remained unanswered. A movement at the side of the house made her catch her breath. The other officer reappeared to inform her that the back door was locked and there was no sign of movement inside the house when he had peered through the kitchen and dining room windows.

"Let's break it down. We've got enough on the suspect to go ahead with no need to get a warrant." Sam stood back as the men took it in turns to shoulder the door. Eventually, it gave way, allowing them access.

"Hey, what the hell is going on down there?" a neighbour shouted from his bedroom window.

Sam stood back to talk to him. She showed her ID, not that the man could see it from that distance. "Sorry to wake you up, sir. We're the police. We were hoping to speak with David Price. I don't suppose you've seen him lately, have you?"

"Yes, he was here earlier. Pulled up at around eight and was gone again by eight-thirty, or thereabouts."

"Did you speak to him? Did he mention where he was going?"

"No, we're not on speaking terms. He damaged the fence in the back garden and refused to contribute to the repairs. What's he done?"

"We're investigating a significant case in which we consider him to be the prime suspect."

"Hey, hang on a minute, you're that copper who was on the telly the other day, aren't you? A kidnapping case as far as I can remember, wasn't it?"

"That's correct. Sorry, I'd love to hang around and have a chat about this, but time is against us and we're desperate to find him."

"I bet you are. He's always come across as a bit of a perv. I've caught him eyeing up the girls from the secondary school up the road. Never hides the fact, either. Good job my daughter is older and he's never looked like that at her, otherwise I would have ripped him apart with my bare hands. He's scum through and through, that one. I'm not surprised you're tagging him as a suspect in that crime you highlighted on the box the other day."

"Do you know if he has access to any other properties in the area?"

"Have you tried his parents' house? He spends a lot of time over there, when he's talking to them."

"Are you saying they have a problematic relationship?"

"You tell me. All I can say is the air turns blue now and again when the three of them are sitting in the garden together."

"Do you mean they argue a lot?"

"Yep, I think one such row ended up with his father going to A and E with a broken nose."

"Is that right? Thanks for the information. One last question and I'll let you get back to the land of Nod."

"And what might that be?"

"Do you know what car he was using?"

"Sorry, I took little notice, except that it wasn't his usual one. If that helps?"

"Colour, make perhaps, or am I pushing it?"

"Red." He chewed his lip for a second or two. "Might have been a BMW, but don't quote me on it."

"That's fantastic. Thanks for all your help. Sorry to have disturbed you."

"All's well that ends well, or doesn't, in this case. I hope you find the bastard and soon. Want me to give your lot a call if he shows up here again?"

"That would be brilliant. Thanks very much."

He smiled tautly and shut the window.

Reluctantly, Sam turned away from the front door and said, "We might as well call it a day. I was going to suggest putting surveillance on the property, but I think the neighbour will stick to his word and call the station if Price comes back here."

The three walked back to the cars. Sam had a brief chat with the officers, thanking them for accompanying her, and slipped into the passenger seat next to her fiancé.

"Should I ask how it went or give it a miss?"

"I'd rather swerve that discussion. Let's get back to the station. We're limited in what we can do right now, but I can make some preparations before we leave tonight."

Rhys stifled a yawn. "Sounds intriguing."

"I feel guilty, you being out here with me. You should be at home, tucked up in bed."

"I'm fine. This is the most excitement I've had in decades."

She inclined her head and groaned. "You might want to reconsider that statement, given recent events."

"Ah yeah. I'll just keep my mouth shut and make myself useful instead." He started the car.

"Yep, you should."

12

Sam should have been tired after getting home at the back end of two, but she was far from it. She left Rhys curled up in bed with Sonny and Casper on the floor, happily snoring alongside him, and snuck out of the house at eight the following morning. No doubt she would pay for her lack of sleep later, but for now, with the adrenaline pumping around her body, she was eager to get on with her day. So much so that she skipped breakfast and her morning coffee before getting on the road.

The café she enjoyed going to for a quick bacon roll proved to be too much of a temptation to ignore as she approached it. She parked up, entered the café and placed her order. Within a matter of minutes, her coffee was served, and shortly after, her bacon roll arrived. Sam tucked into it, suddenly feeling ravenous when the aroma of the sizzling bacon hit her with full force.

While having breakfast, she made a note of how she envisioned her morning starting once she reached the station.

Ten minutes later, she sat back and patted her stomach and stuck up a thumb of appreciation to the chef behind the counter, who always glanced up, seeking the customers' approval.

She got back in the car and set off. Bob was parking in a space next to hers when she arrived. She beeped her horn. He spun around, ready to give the driver a mouthful until he realised who it was. He shook his fist instead, and she got out of the car, laughing.

"Sorry, I couldn't resist it. You're early?"

"Only by about fifteen minutes. I figured you'd probably spend the night here or go home and come in early. Glad to see it was the latter. You need your rest. How did you get on? Did you arrest the bastard?"

"Regrettably not. I'll tell you all about it later, when the others arrive. You know how much I detest repeating myself."

"Christ, not even a hint as to what went on?"

"Not even a hint." She strode off ahead of him and entered the station.

Once upstairs he made another effort to get the information from her, but she swiftly shut him down.

"I want to get my paperwork out of the way before the morning meeting. Feel free to bring me in a coffee at your convenience."

"Glad to see I still have my uses around here," he muttered grumpily.

She pulled a face at him and cracked on with emptying her inbox and her in-tray. Bob graced her with his presence and a coffee ten minutes later and left the office without saying a word. She didn't have to be Einstein to know that he was pissed off with her. She continued with her task until her partner came in a second time to let her know that the rest of the team had arrived and that everyone was eager to hear how the previous evening had gone down.

To ensure the team listened to what she had to say without being distracted, Sam ordered them all to switch off their computers. After she'd finished recapping, she said, "So, folks, what we need to do this morning is hit the ground running. Before I left last night, or should I say, in the early hours of this morning, I set up the usual alerts on the system regarding the airports and the ports. Claire, can you check if anything has come from that ASAP?"

Claire raised her thumb.

"Oliver and Liam, I need you to work together and check the

CCTV footage, if there is any available close to Price's house. His home is on the edge of Workington, so I'm hopeful there might be something out there."

"Leave it with us, boss."

She glanced up at the clock on the wall. It was nine-thirty. "Okay, I'm going to get in touch with Emily and the other women. Check everything is okay at the hotel before I do anything else today."

"And what about me?" Bob asked.

"Can you check in with Nick for me? See if any of the patrols reported anything suspicious involving a red Audi overnight."

"An Audi? I thought you said it was a BMW he took off in?"

She tapped the side of her head. "You're right, you'll have to forgive any slip-ups I make today."

He gave her one of his are-you-shitting-me kind of looks and rose from his seat. "I'll pop down and see for myself."

Ignoring his grumpiness, she returned to her office and rang Emily at the hotel. "Hi, I didn't wake you, did I?"

"No, I've just had a shower. Did you find him? I bet he came up with a crappy cock-and-bull story about why he was holding us captive."

Sam closed her eyes, sensing the woman was about to explode when she delivered the unwanted news. "I'm sorry, he got away."

"He what? Was he still at the house?"

"No. He must have had a spare key on him. The house was empty when we got there."

"Jesus, holy shit! We never thought to check his pockets. Where do we go from here? The woman at reception told us we had to vacate our rooms by ten. We can't go home, can we? Not with him on the bloody loose. We should have killed the fucker when we had the chance." Emily rattled the questions off one after the other, not giving Sam the chance to answer them.

"I need you to remain calm, Emily. Getting worked up won't help. The reason I'm telling you before the others is because I think you're the one who is the most level-headed and capable of hearing the news as it is."

Emily took a couple of steadying breaths. "Okay, I'm getting there. Sorry for overreacting. Can you tell me what happened?"

Sam revealed the details of how the trip to Price's parents' house had panned out and what had occurred at the suspect's home afterwards.

"Shit! What does all of this mean? That we're going to spend the rest of our lives looking over our shoulders in case he's stalking us?"

"I hope that won't be the case. Let's see what today brings, first. I have no intention of letting you ladies down. If he's out there, we're going to do everything we can to bring him in."

"Where does that leave us? With no place to go?"

"I could suggest you all come back to the station for your protection."

"How practical would that be?"

"You're right, not very practical at all. Can you leave it with me for about half an hour? I'll see if I can come up with something more appropriate."

"Just be aware of the time, Sam. Ten o'clock is just around the corner."

"Don't worry. It was a conservative estimate. I have something up my sleeve. I'll get back to you shortly." Sam ended the call and immediately rang the press officer. "Hi, it's Sam Cobbs. Sorry to be a pain in the butt, Jackie, but I could do with your help. Actually, I have two things in mind."

"One not good enough for you these days, is that it?" Jackie chuckled.

"I've got a dilemma on my hands and I'm hoping you can help me out."

"I'll do my best. Shoot!"

"The good news is the four women who were kidnapped are now safe, but the bad news is the suspect is still out there, on the run, although we know who he is."

"Let me guess, at least part of your dilemma is that you need to run another appeal for the suspect. How am I doing so far?"

"Bloody marvellous. How about it?"

"I can get that sorted for you ASAP. But I'm puzzled how I can help you out with the second part of your dilemma."

"I put the women up in a hotel overnight for their own safety, but they need to vacate their rooms by no later than ten this morning because the hotel is fully booked today."

"Right, and?"

"At short notice and, off the top of my head, I came up with the idea that we could use the anteroom, keep them there until we arrest the suspect."

"That's highly unusual, Sam. Why can't they go home?"

"Because the suspect knows where they all live, he's had access to their personal information."

"Dare I ask how?"

"He's a dentist. Turns out all the girls are his patients, furthermore, they went to school with him, so there's a lot of history between them. I wouldn't ask normally, but I was the one who rang all the hotels in the area yesterday and I know they're all chocka. It's either bring them back here or send them home. If we plump for the latter, the suspect being on the loose means he's likely to track them down. Does that even make sense? I was working until two this morning."

"Shit, you're nuts. You shouldn't be at work, Sam. All right, I've got no objection to them using the room during the day, but I can't give you the authority you need to let them stay down there overnight. I'd say you're going to need to run it past DCI Armstrong."

Sam expelled a louder groan than she'd bargained for. "Bugger, I was hoping to keep this between us, for now."

"If you're willing to take the blame in case the plan goes tits up?"

"Of course I will."

"Bring them in then. I'll get another conference sorted."

Sam let out a relieved sigh. "I knew you wouldn't let me down. You're a pal, Jackie."

"I'll get back to you soon."

Sam hung up and rang Emily back straight away. "Hi, it's Sam. I've arranged for you to spend the day here, in the anteroom. It'll give me time to make other arrangements for you, knowing that you're at the station, where Price can't touch you."

"Wow, it's not ideal, but thank you. We appreciate you looking out for us, Sam. I'll let the others know."

"I'll arrange for a couple of patrol cars to pick you up at ten."

"Great, thanks so much."

"I'll see you later. Take care, Emily." She sat back and closed her eyes for a moment.

A knock on the door startled her.

"Were you asleep?" Bob asked.

"No, I don't think so." She rubbed at her eyes, thankful she hadn't applied any mascara before leaving home. "What's up?"

"Claire's got something of interest for you."

Sam shot out of her chair and followed him. Claire wiggled her eyebrows at Sam as she crossed the room to speak to the sergeant. "I know that look. Tell me you have some good news for me."

"I have. Price is booked on a flight to Spain at five this afternoon."

Sam's pulse raced. "Really? Which airport?"

"Manchester," Claire replied.

"This is the best news ever. He's obviously planning to stay with his parents." Her mind reeled. "I need to get in touch with Manchester Police and ask if they can assist us."

"Aren't we going to make the arrest?" Bob asked.

"Let's just cover our backs. It'll be out of our jurisdiction. I was at the Police Academy with an inspector down there. All I have to do now is think of his damn name. It was a strange one. Nelson, that's it, Hero Nelson."

Bob's mouth gaped open.

"Don't ask," Sam said. "I think his mother must have had a sense of humour."

"No kidding. Fancy naming your son Hero and then him choosing to be a copper."

"Behave. I'll call him and see if he can help us out."

. . .

THREE HOURS LATER, two cars set off from the station. Sam allowed Bob to drive her car while she caught up on her sleep, exhausted after holding another appeal with the journalists. Liam and Oliver followed them in Oliver's car. At three-thirty, they met up with DI Hero Nelson, who was accompanied by two male members of his team. He seemed pleased to see Sam again. He hadn't changed in the slightest.

"You're still as handsome as ever, Hero. I can't thank you enough for being up for this."

"Get out of here. You haven't changed a bit, Sam. I'm happy to oblige if it prevents another scumbag criminal escaping the country and setting up home in Spain. He sounds a right charmer."

"Let's hope the facial recognition equipment doesn't let us down around here."

"How do you want to play this? You're in charge, despite it being on my patch."

Sam smiled and punched him gently on the arm. "Really? You're great. I knew I was right to ignore what the others used to say about you at the academy."

Hero rolled his eyes, and the others tittered. "Let's get on with it. I reckon the check-in will be open now if the flight is at five."

"Why don't we find the security room, run it past the guys there, see if they can help us locate him?" Sam suggested.

"Excellent idea. Have you got a photo of the suspect?"

Sam scrolled through her phone to the photo she had downloaded from Price's Facebook page and passed her mobile to Hero.

"Looks a shitty weasel. Can you forward me a copy and I'll pass it on to my men?"

Sam did as instructed, then Hero issued orders to his men and to Sam's team to head over to the check-in area. He also told them to split up, act casual, but remain vigilant as they surveyed the crowd.

Hero pointed towards the reception desk. "We'll ask over there."

Sam struggled to keep up with his long strides, and he reached the desk before she did. He showed his ID and asked to speak to someone in security. The receptionist picked up the phone and contacted a colleague who appeared behind them a few moments later.

Hero explained the situation to the guard. He gave a brief nod and asked them to follow him to a room fifty feet away.

Once they'd entered the room, the guard said, "I'm Rick, this is Isaac."

His colleague remained focused on the screen in front of him.

"We're after this suspect. DI Cobbs is a colleague of mine from Cumbria. We believe the suspect is fleeing the country rather than face up to the crimes he's committed. Earlier this week, he kidnapped four women, held them hostage for a couple of days, and he also ran one of their friends down, putting her in the ICU, where she remains today."

"Let's see what we can do for you. You say he's booked on the five o'clock flight to Barcelona?"

"That's right. Do you have facial recognition equipment here?"

"I think we were one of the first airports to implement it in the UK." He moved over to another desk and angled the screen their way.

Sam spent the next ten minutes flicking between the two screens as if she was at Wimbledon, watching a fast rally on the ultimate day. "I can't see him. Can you?" she asked Hero.

He withdrew his phone from his pocket to refresh his memory of what the suspect looked like. "No, I can't see him at all."

Sam rang her partner. "Have you spotted him, Bob?"

"Nope. What about facial recognition? Do they have that here?"

"We're on it now. Nothing is showing up so far."

"He might be wearing a disguise, so I wouldn't look for the obvious."

"We'll bear that in mind. Get back to me if you spot him."

"Ditto," Bob replied before she ended the call.

"He's got to be here somewhere. Maybe we're searching in the wrong place," Sam said.

Hero leaned forward and peered at the screen showing the passengers in the selected area. "We're not. This is the check-in area for all flights."

"I wonder if he's checked in yet."

Rick picked up the phone on his desk and made the call. "Katherine, it's Rick. Has a passenger by the name of David Price booked in yet? He's on the flight to Barcelona, scheduled to take off at five... that's great, thanks." He hung up and shook his head. "He's not booked in yet."

"Bugger, that means we're searching the wrong area," Sam said and immediately rang Bob back. "He's not checked in for his flight yet. Can you widen the search? Take Oliver and Liam with you."

"Roger that."

After tucking her phone in her pocket, Sam said, "I've got a feeling he's going to leave it until the last minute to appear."

"I know I would," Hero agreed.

"Isaac, can you broaden the search on the cameras for the officers?" Rick asked.

The camera shifted location to the reception area. "I'll keep an eye on this side if you watch the left for me," Sam suggested.

She watched the mixture of excited and the not-so-excited passengers milling around the large reception area. Some choosing to take a seat, obviously too early for their check-in times, and others who left their luggage with family members while they used the facilities in the corner. She watched a young couple having a blazing row before the woman in her early twenties started crying and ran into the loo.

"What it is to be young and full of angst," she said.

"What's that?"

"Nothing, just people watching and being grateful that I'm twenty years older these days."

Hero laughed. "I get days like that, too."

Sam's gaze wandered to the wider area and then back to the toilets. She saw the young woman emerge only to be given the cold shoulder by her boyfriend or husband. It was then her gaze was drawn to a woman with long blonde hair entering the toilets. There was something odd about her that Sam couldn't put her finger on.

Taking a punt, she asked, "Any chance you can take the footage back a little, Isaac?"

"Yep, let me know how long and which area."

Sam shifted closer to the screen. "Outside the ladies' about two minutes ago."

Hero moved to stand beside her. "What have you seen?"

"A woman who looks a bit odd. Bear with me. She wasn't walking straight. I'm probably talking a load of shit. There, that's her." Sam tapped the screen.

The four of them watched in silence as the woman, carrying two holdalls, came through the main entrance and went directly to the toilets.

"You're right, she's either stopped off at the pub on her way here or she's wearing shoes that seem unfamiliar to her," Hero said.

"Can you flip back, Isaac? Let's see what she does when she comes out."

They waited for five minutes or more, but the woman failed to appear. "I'm not liking this. She's been in there too long."

Rick turned to the other machine and ran the footage featuring the woman through it. "Shit. That's him, dressed as a frigging woman."

"I knew it. Fuck, we need to get down there before he fools us with another disguise." She flew out of the door with Hero right behind her.

"Slow down, Sam. The last thing we want to do is spook him."

"You're right. I'm going in there." She didn't wait for Hero to respond. Inside, there were around ten cubicles. She passed by most of them. Five were empty, and the others were all occupied. Sam removed a lipstick from her pocket and stood in front of the mirror. From there, she had a bird's-eye view of all the cubicles.

One by one, the doors opened until a woman with brown hair came out of the last toilet. Sam kept a close eye on her. She had her head down and refused to make eye contact with anyone. She walked up to the hand basin and washed her hands.

Sam noticed a few nicks in the woman's hand, which seemed

larger than normal. "I can't wait to take off. It's the hanging around at the airport that I detest the most, don't you?" Sam tried to strike up a conversation with the woman who ignored her. Sam applied her lipstick and left. She spotted Hero lingering a few feet away and coughed to gain his attention, thumbed behind her and moved out of the way in case the woman, or who she presumed to be Price, suspected her of being anything other than another passenger. She was willing for Hero to swoop in and make the arrest.

The second Price stepped out of the ladies' he saw Hero, dropped his holdalls and legged it. Sam rang Bob and shouted for the surrounding crowd to stand where they were. Of course, the public, fearing that something dangerous was going down, scattered and got between Hero and the absconding Price.

Sam rang her partner. "Bob, where are you?"

"Over by the escalators. What the fuck is going on over there?"

"He's here. Dressed as a woman with brunette hair in the style of a bob, err... you know what I mean. Can you see him?"

"I can see Hero chasing someone. Don't worry, we'll close in on him. I'll give Liam and Oliver a call. Price is heading towards them."

"Tell them to be careful. I'm on my way."

Sam removed her shoes and sprinted after Hero, dodging the odd horrified passenger en route. She was too vertically challenged to see if Hero was catching up with the suspect or not. She kept her fingers crossed as she continued the chase across the cold tiled reception area in her stockinged feet. A large man, wearing a straw hat and string vest, suddenly stepped in her path. She connected with his rotund frame, bounced backwards and ended up on the floor.

A woman rushed forward to help her to her feet. "I'm so sorry. He never looks where he's going."

Sam smiled at the woman and took up her pursuit. The crowd parted in front of her, and she came to a grinding halt. There, standing ahead of her, was Price, his wig removed, being held on either side by Hero and Bob, a smug expression on each of their faces. Thank God for that!

She approached them, and Hero said, "He didn't get very far. Nice try, though."

"Screw you, I've escaped before. I'll do it again," Price sneered.

"Have you read him his rights?" Sam said.

Hero smiled. "I thought I'd leave that honour to you."

After Sam cautioned the suspect, he spat at her feet and said, "It was all worth it to see the fear etched on those bitches' faces."

"Ah, maybe, but they're the ones who have had the last laugh. No wonder you've taken to wearing a wig. You must have a decent-sized lump on the back of your head from where Rachel whacked you with a hammer. Get him out of my sight. Oliver, you and Liam can have the pleasure of his company on the way back to Cumbria."

Sam and Bob watched their colleagues steer Price through the reception area and out to the car.

Sam turned to Hero and shook his hand. "Thanks for all your help, Hero. It's been great meeting up with you again after all these years. If ever you're up our way, drop by and see me."

"Well, then, there's an offer I can't refuse. I'm glad things turned out for the best. Men like him make my bloody skin crawl."

"I agree. Right, partner, we'd better get on the road. You can drive. I've got a few calls to make on the way."

"General dogsbody and chauffeur, that's all I am these days," Bob complained.

"Ignore him. He's always whinging about something or other. Thanks again, Hero."

"You make a good team, that's what matters at the end of the day. I've had my fill of dubious partners over the years, but we won't go there."

Sam laughed while Bob stared at Hero. The three of them left the building together and reached the vehicles just as Oliver was pulling out, and the look Price gave them would have frozen hell over in seconds.

"Tosser. I hope the CPS throws the book at him," Bob said.

"They will, if I have anything to do with it," Sam added.

They said farewell to Hero a last time and then got on the road.

Sam rang the station and spoke with Emily. "Hi, it's Sam. Are the others listening?"

"Yes, we're all here. Please tell me you've found him?"

"We have. He's been arrested, and he's on his way back to Cumbria."

A loud cheer broke out from Emily and her friends. A couple of them even broke down and sobbed. "Thank God for that. Does this mean we can go home?"

"You can. He won't escape again. You have my word. Can you pass me back to the desk sergeant?"

"Yes, thank you so much to you and your team, Inspector."

"Don't forget we had a deal, Emily."

"I won't. I'll have a word with my boss tomorrow and get back to you. Here's the desk sergeant now."

She handed the phone over, and Nick came on the line. "Yes, ma'am?"

"Can you ensure the women get home safely, Nick?"

"Of course. I'll make the arrangements right away."

"Thanks. We'll be back in a few hours."

"Drive safely."

Sam ended the call and rang the station back to inform the rest of the team, who were obviously thrilled by the result. She also insisted they go home at the normal time. Claire tried to argue with her, but Sam won in the end. Then she threw her phone into her lap and expelled a satisfying breath.

"It's ironic, isn't it?" Bob asked.

"What is?"

"That he dressed up as a woman, frigging dickhead. I mean him, not you. Do you reckon he was intending to do a quick change before his flight?"

"Probably, especially if the ticket was in his name." Then Sam laughed until she cried, mainly from sheer exhaustion.

"What are you laughing at? It's not that funny," he grumbled.

Eventually, she drifted off to sleep, and Bob nudged her to wake her up at the other end.

"Wake up, Sleeping Beauty, we're here."

"Gosh, that was quick."

"Nope, around three hours, as usual. You were zonked out most of the way."

He drew up next to her car. Sam got out, yawned and stretched the knots out of her neck and back. She detested the sound of the clicking, aware of how old that made her seem.

"Everything all right over there?"

"Yep. Let's get the bastard charged and head home for the night. It's been a long day."

"Phew, I thought you were going to tell me you intended to grill him this evening."

"No, I want him to experience what it's like to be put in a cell overnight, see how he likes it."

"He'd better get used to it, and quickly. I reckon he's got at least twenty years coming his way, if not more."

"Hopefully, it'll be a lot more than that, especially if Emily comes up trumps for us."

"Maybe journalists have their uses after all."

"I'm yet to be convinced. Ask me what I think after she's handed over the evidence she's collected, if her boss is agreeable to it."

"There's always a stumbling block to things like this, isn't there?"

"Yep, nothing is plain sailing. Everything has to be achieved the hard way, but we should be used to that by now. Let's go process the bastard. At least we can take some satisfaction in knowing that we prevented him from leaving the country. He tried to outsmart us but wasn't clever enough to pull it off in the end."

EPILOGUE

Sam was eager to get to work the next morning. Rhys insisted on getting up with her, to make her a substantial breakfast in case she didn't get around to having any lunch during her busy schedule.

"You're an idiot. You needn't have done this for me."

"Nonsense. I did it for both of us. I'm going to make the most of the wonderful weather. By that I mean, it's dry out there and the rain is due to hit us tomorrow and last for a few days."

"Where are you going this time?"

"I thought I might take the dogs over to Coniston. I've always wanted to visit it, and now that the famous Bluebird K7 is back where it belongs after a twenty-three-year absence, I thought I might take a look at it."

Sam wasn't sure how to react. On the one hand, she wanted Rhys to get out there by himself to help regain his confidence. However, on the other, it was a trip she was hoping they'd make together. She said nothing, just continued to tuck in to her scrambled eggs and bacon.

"Say something," he said. "You don't think it's a good idea, do you?"

"No, no, no, that's not why I'm quiet. All right, I'm delighted you want to go over there by yourself..."

"I sense a *but* coming."

"I thought it might be a trip we made together, maybe in the spring."

"God, I'm a selfish idiot. Of course, I'll postpone it and go with your idea because it would be a much better day out if we went together."

"You needn't wait. Damn, I shouldn't have said anything. I'm sorry."

He smiled. "There's no need. I'll get the map out, stick closer to home, and we'll see the historic hydroplane together."

"Thank you. That'll be something for us to look forward to."

"We should sit down and make more plans like that for the future, because, let's face it, none of us know what's in store for us, do we?"

"Ain't that the truth? Maybe we can do that at the weekend. Are you going to accompany me to the funeral on Friday?"

"Are you asking me to be your plus-one?"

She cringed. "Is that something you say about a funeral?"

"Sorry, I was trying to make a joke and ended up making a huge faux pas instead."

"You're forgiven." She ate the last mouthful of her breakfast and pushed back her chair. "I'll do the washing-up before I go."

"You will not. I can do that before the boys and I head off for our walk."

"You're such a good man. Thanks, Rhys."

"And here's a snippet of news that I think will brighten your day further. I'm going back to work on Monday."

She leaned in for a kiss. "That's excellent news."

"It's all down to you. If you hadn't allowed me to tag along with you the other night, I'd still be wrapped up in self-pity instead of pushing myself to face the realities of life again."

"I'm delighted my plan worked."

"What? You did it on purpose?"

"Someone had to give you a kick up the backside. You weren't having much success doing it yourself, were you?" She kissed him again, amused by his gobsmacked expression.

"You can be so devious at times."

She winked at him. "Never underestimate a woman copper, especially an inspector."

"I'll bear that in mind. What do you think the outcome will be today?"

"I have every confidence that Price will go down the 'no comment' route, so it's up to us to show him the evidence we have against him and go from there."

"Well, good luck, not that you'll need it."

"Thanks. I'll call you later, time permitting. Enjoy your day with the munchkins." She bent down to kiss first Sonny and then Casper on the head.

DURING THE INTERVIEW, Price either stared at Sam through eyes full of hatred or at the wall behind her, spouting two words to each of her questions: no comment. She called a halt to the interview about an hour later and ordered the uniformed officer at the back of the room to take Price back to his cell. His sinister laugh echoed through the corridor, sending shivers down Sam's spine.

Sam and Bob returned to the incident room.

"As expected, he failed to answer any of my questions. What we need to do now is ensure we have all the evidence against him tied up in a neat bow ready for the CPS. Let's see how far we can get with all of that today, folks, before another case comes our way."

"What about Emily? Have you heard from her yet?" Claire asked.

"No, I said I'd leave it a couple of days, but I must admit, the longer I leave it, the more anxious it's making me feel. Thanks for the prompt. I think I'll call her now."

"I'll bring you in a coffee," Bob volunteered.

She walked through to her office to place the call. "Hi, Emily, it's Sam Cobbs. Can you talk?"

"In a second, let me change rooms." Footsteps sounded, and a door squeaked. "Sorry, you know what it's like around here. How are you? I've been meaning to call you. I was holding off because I thought you might be busy interviewing Price."

"I'm doing okay. We've interviewed him, and it won't come as a surprise to you when I tell you he went down the 'no comment' route. Even though I presented the evidence against him. Any news from your end?"

"Yes and no, I ran it past my boss, and he's debating whether to hand over the evidence I have on Price at the moment."

"Do I need to force his hand? I will if I have to."

"I've already warned him about that. Let me keep working on him for a few days. You know how stubborn editors can be."

"So I've heard. How are you and the other girls? Have you made it up with them yet?"

"Sort of. They're trying to come to terms with the fact that none of this was my fault, but it's going to take time for them to forgive me."

"Stick with it. I'm sure they'll come around. Have you all given your statements?"

"Yes. Some of them were putting it off, but I had a word, emphasised how important it was to ensure he gets put away, otherwise, if he walked free there would only be one thing on his agenda."

"Ouch, I bet that went down well with them."

"Not really, but they're foolish to believe that if they sit back and do nothing at all, this will go away. You and I know differently, don't we?"

"We do. Okay, can you get back to me within forty-eight hours?"

"I promise. Thanks again for all you did for us, Sam."

"That's what we're here for. Any help you journalists will give us along the way is an added bonus."

"I know. I'll do my best for you. Oh, I forgot to tell you, I rang the hospital this morning. They told me Amy has regained consciousness."

"That's fantastic news."

. . .

Friday morning arrived and, dressed all in black, Sam and Rhys headed off to the church in Workington, where the service was due to be held. They met up with the rest of the team, who had opted to attend the service without their partners.

"I feel like a spare part now," Rhys whispered as they walked towards Bob and the others.

"Don't be silly. I'm glad you're here with me. I think those must be Alex's kids over there. I'd better pay my respects. I won't be long." She tapped Bob on the shoulder. "Do you want to join me?" Sam gestured towards the group of youngsters gathered behind them.

"Not really," he muttered.

"Come on. I could do with you being by my side. You knew him better than I did."

"That's debatable. All right, let's get this over with."

The group saw them approaching, and a young man in his late twenties stepped forward with his hand out, ready for Sam to shake.

"Are you Nigel?" Sam asked.

"That's right, and I'm assuming you're Dad's boss, DI Cobbs."

"Call me Sam. I'm so sorry for your loss. Your father was a good man, an integral part of our team. We will all miss his wicked sense of humour around the office." She could feel Bob glance her way but ignored him.

He smiled and nodded. "He had a dark sense of humour. I'm surprised you got it. Most of us struggled with it."

"I'm glad you could all make it. He spoke fondly of you all." Another lie, but only a white one that she felt was allowed under the circumstances.

"We loved him, although it was hard at times. We made sure one of us spoke with him every week. We tried to persuade him to come home to Scotland, even though none of us knew he had a heart problem. He was adamant he wanted to stay here and continue to work with you guys."

Hearing that brought unexpected tears to her eyes. "We will miss him."

The vicar appeared and asked everyone to take their seat inside the church. Sam held Rhys' hand throughout the service. His presence made her realise how lucky she was to still have him after his life-threatening ordeal.

After the service was held, the congregation moved to the graveside. The coffin was lowered into the hole and, as his children scattered earth on Alex's coffin, one by one, Alex spoke to them.

The first knock on the coffin had startled them all. Sheer terror filled every one of them. But it was Nigel who laughed first as his father's words filled the area via a recorded message.

"It's dark in here. Who turned out the lights? Let me out. It's not time for me to sign out yet."

Sam fell into Rhys' arms and cried, this time with laughter. As her laughter died down, the shame set in. "I never knew him at all, not really. Fancy him putting us through this, what a wicked sense of humour he must have had."

"Don't stress about it. He loved being a member of your team, Sam. Take heart from that."

"You're right, I know. RIP Alex Dougall, you will be missed by all of us."

THE END

THANK you for reading To Fear Him, the next thrilling adventure is To Deceive Them.

While you're waiting for that to come out, have you read any of my other fast-paced crime thrillers yet?

WHY NOT TRY the first book in the DI Sara Ramsey series
No Right To Kill

. . .

OR GRAB the first book in the bestselling, award-winning, Justice series here, Cruel Justice

OR THE FIRST book in the spin-off Justice Again series, Gone in Seconds

PERHAPS YOU'D PREFER to try one of my other police procedural series, the DI Kayli Bright series which begins with The Missing Children

OR MAYBE YOU'D enjoy the DI Sally Parker series set in Norfolk, Wrong Place

OR MY GRITTY police procedural starring DI Nelson set in Manchester, Torn Apart

OR MAYBE YOU'D like to try one of my successful psychological thrillers I know The Truth or She's Gone or Shattered Lives

KEEP IN TOUCH WITH M A COMLEY

Newsletter
http://smarturl.it/8jtcvv

BookBub
www.bookbub.com/authors/m-a-comley

Blog
http://melcomley.blogspot.com

Facebook Readers' Page
https://www.facebook.com/groups/2498593423507951

TikTok
https://www.tiktok.com/@melcomley

ALSO BY M A COMLEY

Blind Justice (Novella)

Cruel Justice (Book #1)

Mortal Justice (Novella)

Impeding Justice (Book #2)

Final Justice (Book #3)

Foul Justice (Book #4)

Guaranteed Justice (Book #5)

Ultimate Justice (Book #6)

Virtual Justice (Book #7)

Hostile Justice (Book #8)

Tortured Justice (Book #9)

Rough Justice (Book #10)

Dubious Justice (Book #11)

Calculated Justice (Book #12)

Twisted Justice (Book #13)

Justice at Christmas (Short Story)

Prime Justice (Book #14)

Heroic Justice (Book #15)

Shameful Justice (Book #16)

Immoral Justice (Book #17)

Toxic Justice (Book #18)

Overdue Justice (Book #19)

Unfair Justice (a 10,000 word short story)

Irrational Justice (a 10,000 word short story)

Seeking Justice (a 15,000 word novella)

Caring For Justice (a 24,000 word novella)

Savage Justice (a 17,000 word novella)

Justice at Christmas #2 (a 15,000 word novella)

Gone in Seconds (Justice Again series #1)

Ultimate Dilemma (Justice Again series #2)

Shot of Silence (Justice Again series #3)

Taste of Fury (Justice Again series #4)

Crying Shame (Justice Again series #5)

See No Evil (Justice Again series #6)

To Die For (DI Sam Cobbs #1)

To Silence Them (DI Sam Cobbs #2)

To Make Them Pay (DI Sam Cobbs #3)

To Prove Fatal (DI Sam Cobbs #4)

To Condemn Them (DI Sam Cobbs #5)

To Punish Them (DI Sam Cobbs #6)

To Entice Them (DI Sam Cobbs #7)

To Control Them (DI Sam Cobbs #8)

To Endanger Lives (DI Sam Cobbs #9)

To Hold Responsible (DI Sam Cobbs #10)

To Catch a Killer (DI Sam Cobbs #11)

To Believe the Truth (DI Sam Cobbs #12)

To Blame Them (DI Sam Cobbs 13)

To Judge Them (DI Sam Cobbs #14)

To Fear Him (DI Sam Cobbs #15)

To Deceive Them (DI Sam Cobbs #16)

Forever Watching You (DI Miranda Carr thriller)

Wrong Place (DI Sally Parker thriller #1)

No Hiding Place (DI Sally Parker thriller #2)

Cold Case (DI Sally Parker thriller#3)

Deadly Encounter (DI Sally Parker thriller #4)
Lost Innocence (DI Sally Parker thriller #5)
Goodbye My Precious Child (DI Sally Parker #6)
The Missing Wife (DI Sally Parker #7)
Truth or Dare (DI Sally Parker #8)
Where Did She Go? (DI Sally Parker #9)
Sinner (DI Sally Parker #10)
The Good Die Young (DI Sally Parker #11)
Coping Without You (DI Sally Parker #12)
Could It Be Him (DI Sally Parker #13)
Frozen In Time (DI Sally Parker #14)
Echoes of Silence (DI Sally Parker #15)
Web of Deceit (DI Sally Parker Novella)
The Missing Children (DI Kayli Bright #1)
Killer On The Run (DI Kayli Bright #2)
Hidden Agenda (DI Kayli Bright #3)
Murderous Betrayal (Kayli Bright #4)
Dying Breath (Kayli Bright #5)
Taken (DI Kayli Bright #6)
The Hostage Takers (DI Kayli Bright Novella)
No Right to Kill (DI Sara Ramsey #1)
Killer Blow (DI Sara Ramsey #2)
The Dead Can't Speak (DI Sara Ramsey #3)
Deluded (DI Sara Ramsey #4)
The Murder Pact (DI Sara Ramsey #5)
Twisted Revenge (DI Sara Ramsey #6)
The Lies She Told (DI Sara Ramsey #7)
For The Love Of... (DI Sara Ramsey #8)
Run for Your Life (DI Sara Ramsey #9)

Cold Mercy (DI Sara Ramsey #10)

Sign of Evil (DI Sara Ramsey #11)

Indefensible (DI Sara Ramsey #12)

Locked Away (DI Sara Ramsey #13)

I Can See You (DI Sara Ramsey #14)

The Kill List (DI Sara Ramsey #15)

Crossing The Line (DI Sara Ramsey #16)

Time to Kill (DI Sara Ramsey #17)

Deadly Passion (DI Sara Ramsey #18)

Son of the Dead (DI Sara Ramsey #19)

Evil Intent (DI Sara Ramsey #20)

The Games People Play (DI Sara Ramsey #21)

Revenge Streak (DI Sara Ramsey #22)

Seeking Retribution (DI Sara Ramsey #23)

Gone... But Where? (DI Sara Ramsey #24)

Last Man Standing (DI Sara Ramsey #25)

Vanished (DI Sara Ramsey #26)

I Know The Truth (A Psychological thriller)

She's Gone (A psychological thriller)

Shattered Lives (A psychological thriller)

Evil In Disguise – a novel based on True events

Deadly Act (Hero series novella)

Torn Apart (Hero series #1)

End Result (Hero series #2)

In Plain Sight (Hero Series #3)

Double Jeopardy (Hero Series #4)

Criminal Actions (Hero Series #5)

Regrets Mean Nothing (Hero series #6)

Prowlers (Di Hero Series #7)

Sole Intention (Intention series #1)

Grave Intention (Intention series #2)

Devious Intention (Intention #3)

Cozy mysteries

Murder at the Wedding

Murder at the Hotel

Murder by the Sea

Death on the Coast

Death By Association

Merry Widow (A Lorne Simpkins short story)

It's A Dog's Life (A Lorne Simpkins short story)

A Time To Heal (A Sweet Romance)

A Time For Change (A Sweet Romance)

High Spirits

The Temptation series (Romantic Suspense/New Adult Novellas)

Past Temptation

Lost Temptation

Clever Deception (co-written by Linda S Prather)

Tragic Deception (co-written by Linda S Prather)

Sinful Deception (co-written by Linda S Prather)

Printed in Dunstable, United Kingdom